THE MEETING ON THE
MOON

FReE
JROCK

FRAN CLARK

Library of Congress Cataloging-in-Publication Data

Clark, Fran.

The Meeting On The Moon / Fran Clark – 1st ed.

p. cm.

ISBN 978-0-9914249-2-4

Published by Ocean Water Publishing

Rosenberg, TX

franclark.com

Printed in the United States of America,

PUBLISHER'S NOTE

This a work of fiction. Names, characters, places, and incidents either are the
products of this author's imagination or are used fictitiously. Any resemblance
to actual persons, living or dead, business or religious establishments, events, or
locales is entirely coincidental.

Book design by Fran Clark Photography

To Chip and our beautiful gifts
Clay, Jay, and Meredith

ACKNOWLEDGMENTS

To my dear husband Chip, simply thank you! Without your support, this work would still be a work in progress. I thank and honor you.

I'm eternally grateful to my mother, who consistently modeled reading in my formative years. It sparked my love of reading and planted the writing seed.

To my sweet angels, Clay, Jay, and Meredith, thank you. You give me breath, and provide inspiration for me to see projects to completion. I love you to the moon and back!

Siblings are the best! Thank you Carl, Carol, Darrell, and Rena for loving and promoting your little sister with pride. I wouldn't trade you for the world!

I curtsy before those who graciously lent their eyes to critique the novel during the early phases. You applauded what was good and offered a loving no-no to elements that didn't quite work: Meredith Clark, Jennifer Williams-Adams, Barbara Willis, Vanorda Richardson, and my editor-in-chief, Chip.

Thanks to my friend and writing mentor, author Alexus Rhone. Your character shined as you patiently and selflessly cheered me on, offering invaluable self-publishing advice. Thanks for always showing up, even if you came late and had to sit on the back pew.

Hats off to my adopted little sister, Atrinity Thomas, the musical and creative genius who spent countless hours to inspire the book trailer. Your gifts are amazing, and I thank God for you! Your heart is beautiful!

I want to acknowledge the assistance of my "keepers" who constantly asked "What else can I do to help?" Sherry Dunlap, Marci Henson, Shawn Lemons, Michelle Novosad, Carl Dunlap II, Vickie Maxwell, Merinda and Reggie Martin, and Courtney Williams. I am indebted to you!

To my extended family and friends who prayed for the message and the messenger, I thank you!

Finally, to the Alpha and Omega, the Creator of all that exist, my Sun and my Moon, the One who constantly whispers to me that He loves me unconditionally; my Savior, my Abba...I love you from the bottom of my heart! I'm thankful and humbled that You chose me to deliver this message. I, Your willing vessel, enjoyed the journey. To You be the glory, always and forever.

"Until we have seen someone's darkness,
we don't really know who they are.
Until we have forgiven someone's darkness,
we don't really know what love is."

~ *Marianne Williamson*

Prologue

October 28, 2008

"11-Year-Old Bully Kills Boy At School"

TEXAS — An 11 year old boy has been charged with murder after the beating death of another student in the small town of Solome near Houston, authorities said.

The juvenile suspect, Luke Hermann, is accused of beating to death fellow student Andrew Carmichael Jr. at Sterling Creek Elementary. Carmichael suffered broken ribs and internal bleeding from the brutal bashing that led to his death. The incident occurred during recess. By the time teachers were alerted, it was too late.

Hermann, who reportedly confessed to the assault, was immediately detained by school officials, and was later charged with murder.

Friends of Andrew told reporters that Luke was an angry kid who frequently picked on Andrew, but they didn't know why. One friend described the victim as a straight-A student, great athlete, an avid reader, and was well liked by many of his peers. This murder comes as a big shock to the small town of Solome, TX. Carmichael, who loved science, aspired to one day become an astronaut. He leaves to mourn his parents, Andrew Sr. and Karen Carmichael, and 15 month old sister, Sophia.

Fall 2008

CHAPTER ONE

Will today be the day I die? Drew wondered. *Maybe.* His conscience answered. The time was 12:18pm. Drew's heart rate increased. His legs shook nervously. His teacher, Ms. Crane, kept the temperature in the classroom at a chilly 69 degrees, but sweat formed curiously on his forehead.

I'm not scared! I'm not scared! He told himself.

Yes you are! His conscience fired back. He tried ignoring the voice and pretended that everything was okay. But it wasn't. Everything was not okay.

The clock struck 12:29. His heart raced even faster: THUMP-THUMP... THUMP-THUMP... THUMP-THUMP... THUMP-THUMP. The other 22 students in room 503 were watching the clock too. They stole glances at each other and smiled, as if at 12:30 streamers would fall from the ceiling and a band would burst into Auld Lang Syne to welcome in the New Year. But there was no new year, only a long awaited kickball competition against the other 5th grade classes at Sterling Creek Elementary. It was a longstanding tradition and only one minute stood between them and their anticipated victory. Drew felt dread.

"Alright class, its 12:30! Time to head out! Let's do this!" Ms. Crane announced. The students let out a collective sigh and cheered as they formed a crooked line to head outside. Drew forced a smile as he slowly walked to the end of the line, giving each of his team-mates a sweaty-palmed hi-five. There was no controlling his heart. It had a mind of its own.

They all rushed out to the field, but Drew walked as slow as he could. Ms. Crane even passed him up to get outside.

"Come along now Andrew! We need your help out here!"

"Coming Ms. Crane."

Drew felt sick to his stomach as he approached the double doors. He knew who was waiting for him outside. Someone who meant him no good. He thought about turning and running as fast as he could, but he knew that wasn't an option. He had to face him again. He stepped through the doors and took a few steps. Just as he was about to bolt towards the field to the left, he was yanked by his right arm and quickly pulled to the side of the building where no one could see. The assailant twisted Drew's arm behind his back, and drove his body into the building, scratching the side of his face on the rough brick.

"Well, well, well! Look at my little lab monkey, trying to get away. Listen to me, and listen to me good! You may be good at kickball and all, but you won't be good today. No. You know why? You're gonna sit this game out. Pretend like you're sick or something, because it's our turn to win! You don't want what I did to you last week to happen again, now do you? Remember what happened last week, huh?"

Drew wanted to say, *Go kick dirt! No one's afraid of you!* But he knew it was far from the truth. Besides, his heart was in his throat, preventing any words from escaping.

"If I were you, I wouldn't want that happening again! But just in case you decide to go against my orders... " The bully balled up his fist, and shoved Drew's face into the brick wall with it. "Let this be your reminder. After I'm done with you, you'll be afraid to look at another kickball for the rest of your pathetic life!"

Drew swallowed hard as he attempted to ignore the pain he felt.

"Luke, get your filthy hands off of him right now!" demanded Matthew as he pushed him away from Drew. It wasn't his first time seeing Luke attack his friend. He'd witnessed him kicking Drew in the back the week before, and begged Drew to report him to Ms. Crane. Drew always convinced him that Luke would stop and move on to bully another kid. Matthew went along with it, but when he didn't see the team's star player nor Luke on the field, he knew his best friend was in trouble.

"You listen to me you, you problem child! You'd better keep your hands off of Drew before you're in a heap of trouble! What in the world is wrong with you? Are you mad because Drew is the best kickball player this school has ever seen? Huh? Or are you mad that your class won't ever measure up to ours? It's just a game Luke! Get over yourself and STOP BEING A SORE LOSER!"

Luke's hands were balled in fists, as if preparing to defend himself. The hard square of his jaw became more pronounced as he clenched his teeth. His sandy curls hung messily atop his head while he rocked from side to side in a defensive motion. His hazel eyes stared angrily at Matthew.

"Shut it up Matthew! This is none of your freaking business!"

"It is my business! When you mess with my friend, you mess with me!"

"Well, I tell you what *friend*! When I rearrange his face, I'll be sure to rearrange yours too, Mr. Bodyguard! It'll be sort of like a... like a two for one special! How about that, huh! Or you can just let germ face here defend himself!"

Drew kept his head down, afraid to look up at his opponent. But Matthew didn't back down. He got close to Luke's face, looked him squarely in the eyes and yelled, "Leave him alone!"

Matthew grabbed Drew's arm and pulled him hard in the direction of the kickball field. Drew was relieved for the intervention, but was miserably embarrassed.

"You know Matt, you don't have to always come to my rescue. I can handle Luke all by myself."

"Oh really Drew? Really? Because you were doing a fine job of that when I walked up; only you had the letters H.E.L.P. written on your forehead! If you won't put him in his place, then I don't mind doing it for you. You need to tell on him Drew!" He shook his head in disappointment. "C'mon shake it off, and let's help our class win this game, okay?" Matthew gave him a thumbs up, but Drew was too humiliated to return the sentiment.

Drew's classmates were depending on his skills to help win this game. He was their star, always kicking the ball exactly where it needed to go. Then, he'd follow up with lightning-like speed to first base. He reluctantly played in the game to appease his classmates and Ms. Crane, but decided not to give it his all because of Luke.

He played lousy, but even his worst efforts scored the team points. Class 503 won. His teammates hoisted Drew up in the air as they celebrated one victory down. Drew was paralyzed with fear, as he scanned the field for his bully. There. He found him. Luke was staring up at him, holding a balled fist in front of his own face. Then he pointed his finger towards Drew. Drew swallowed hard, as he looked away, wondering if the word 'fear' was flashing in neon lights on his forehead. Matthew was right, Drew thought. If he wanted to see his next birthday, he'd better tell an adult soon.

CHAPTER TWO

That evening, Drew sat quietly at his desk in his room, reflecting over his long and exhausting day. His mom always told him to focus on positive things. She said it would make him feel better. Well, two good things happened today, he thought. For one, he'd turned in his science project that took three weeks to complete. Then he thought about how he'd assisted his classmates in winning the kickball game. "Okay, maybe just one good thing happened today", he mumbled to himself.

Dad has got to talk to me this time, he thought. For some reason, his father had been acting strange, as if repulsed by being in the same room with Drew. So Drew's past attempts to talk to him had been failures, but he was too desperate to give up. His next attempt had to be different, because his life depended on it. He imagined it to be light conversation that would easily transition into the more serious one. He would tell his dad about Luke the bully, and share how scared he was for his life. His dad would put his arm around his shoulder, then tell him about his own childhood bully, and the clever way he got the bullying to end. The two of them would laugh and come up with a step-by-step plan of how to handle Luke the next day at school. If it failed somehow, his dad would visit the school the next day and address the issue. Drew would thank him, and his dad would give him a hug, assuring him that everything would be fine.

The aroma of dinner entered Drew's room, interrupting his thoughts. It smelled of garlic, onions, and oregano — all the signs of an Italian meal. Lasagna or spaghetti, he thought. If it wasn't ready, it would be soon. So he washed up and rushed down to the dinner table. To his surprise, his parents and baby sister Sophia were already seated and waiting for him. He passed by Sophia's high chair, and landed a kiss on her cheek. She smiled and grabbed for his face, but Drew was too fast for her. He was already seated.

"Hi Dad!" Drew said.

"Hi Drew." Andrew Carmichael, Sr. dryly replied.

"Mom, dinner smells delicious!"

Karen Carmichael had prepared her famous spaghetti with meatballs, a side of garden salad, and garlic bread. Drew admired her as she poured fresh squeezed lemonade into each of their glasses. She was 35 years old and was of average height with a thin frame. She kept her hair dyed black and styled in a medium length bob. She often said the color accentuated her mocha-colored skin and dark brown eyes. She reminded Drew of a particular Hollywood star, always calling her to the television when he saw her. *"Hey mom, come see! Your twin is on T.V."*

"Thanks son! Hope it's as good as it smells!"

Drew looked at his dad, and knew instantly that his next attempt had better be good. The dismal look on his face spoke volumes. He was in one of those funky moods again. Is it me who puts him in these foul moods? Or could it be that he never wanted another child, so every time he sees Sophia, he gets upset? No, that can't be it. He is crazy about his Sophia! Drew shook his head, but decided he'd attempt to snap him out of it anyways.

"Hey Dad, got a funny joke for you!"

His mother interrupted. "Son, say grace first, please."

"Oh, okay. Lord, we thank you for this food that we are about to receive. We ask that you bless it, and let it be nourishment to our bodies. In Jesus' name we pray. Amen."

Maybe the sour look on his face is because he's hungry, Drew decided. He postponed the joke, at least for a few bites.

The only sounds heard at the table were forks hitting against plates, and baby talk from Sophia as she pounded fistfuls of spaghetti against her tray. Drew poked at his food, then pretended to take the fork up to his mouth. The truth was, he had no appetite. It had been replaced weeks ago by sadness and fear.

Halfway through dinner, Drew got up the nerve to break the silence.

"Oh yeah, Dad. Almost forgot about the joke."

"Not in the mood tonight son." He quickly replied.

Drew swallowed hard. Don't give up, he told himself.

"C'mon Dad, I think you'll like it! It's actually pretty funny!" Drew's heart raced.

"Not tonight. Not in the joking mood. Tell me tomorrow."

"Why tomorrow?"

"It's been a long day at work son, that's why. You'll understand when you're my age."

Drew was desperate. He needed his dad to be in a good mood. He longed to talk to him... not tomorrow, but tonight! Drew lost it.

"If your work makes you so tired and sad all the time, then I suggest you quit and get yourself another job, because you're failing at this one!"

"What did you just say to me?"

"Andrew James Carmichael!" yelled his mother. "Don't talk to your father like that! Have some respect! Have you lost your mind?"

Drew was like a train that had left the station and was now traveling at a high rate of speed. He couldn't stop. Not now.

"All I'm trying to do, Mom, is have a normal conversation with this man who calls himself my father! Telling me he's had a long day is just not acceptable, and you know it isn't!"

"Boy!" Karen shot back. Drew interrupted her.

"What if I went to school and told Ms. Crane that I had a long night, and that I wasn't in the mood to do my work? I'd be in trouble, right? Because it's just not acceptable!" Drew looked at his shocked mother then back at his father. He suddenly wished he'd applied the emergency breaks miles back, but it was too late. The train had crashed. There was a sadness in this man's eyes that made no sense. None at all.

Without looking at Drew, his father calmly said, "Son, go to your room."

"Wait, Dad! I'm sorry! I... I don't know what just happened here."

"Go to your room, Drew, before I say or do something to you that I'll regret!"

Drew pushed away from the table in slow motion, then stood fast. *Way to go smart guy! That's the way you get your dad to talk to you!* As he ran up the stairs, he wondered about other possibilities. What if his father was disappointed in him because he heard from Matthew's father that he was a coward at school and wouldn't stand up for himself against a bully? Or worse, maybe his father works with Luke's father and has had to endure jokes about how he is a total wimp. Drew slowly closed his bedroom door, and leaned up against it. He jokingly thought how he should start writing out his will and last testament. He was pretty sure Luke was plotting his death.

Drew showered quickly, slid into his pajama bottoms, then paused in front of the full length mirror that hung on the back of his closet door. He studied himself long and hard. A brown-skinned boy with brown eyes and a low-cut curly afro stared back at him. He faked a smile, revealing his dimpled cheeks, fairly straight teeth, and perfect full lips. His height and size were average for his age of 11. To him, he didn't look like a monster. So what was it that made Luke pick him to bully, and not some other kid? He positioned his arms to make bicep curls. "Just pathetic!" he said. Apparently, that was the reason, he concluded.

He walked away from the mirror with no clear answers. He plopped down beside his bed to say his prayers. It wasn't something his parents required of him. He just did it because it was a practice that his grandparents had taught him.

Maybe I am crazy, he thought. Crazy for talking to someone who doesn't talk back. He lifted himself onto his bed, then laid down. Then he sat up again and slid right back down to assume the kneeling position like before. "Yeah, I'm crazy!" he mumbled. He closed his eyes and started to pray. Somehow talking to this mystery God that he knew little about made him feel better.

"Our Father, who art in Heaven. Hallowed be Thy name... "

After praying, Drew reached over to turn off his lamp then pulled his covers up to his chin. He stared at the ceiling and noticed a soft light entering his room from the window. He smiled! *"It's a full moon tonight!"*

Drew loved the moon, although he was spooked by it when he was three years old. It followed him everywhere he went at night. However, by the time he turned four, he had made peace with this round ball in the sky, thinking of it as a friend that wanted to be everywhere he was. Years passed and the moon became his obsession. Nothing compared to it. He longed for night to come so that he could steal glances at it for as long as he could. He felt a sense of comfort when he saw it—a kind of peace that he could never explain. When asked what he wanted to be when he grew up, the question was a no-brainer. "An astronaut," he would say with pride.

Drew leaped over to his window and drew the curtain open. The moonlight didn't need his permission to enter. They were old friends. It just rushed in and casted a soft glow onto him and the floor. He gazed at the moon and declared "One day, I'll make that journey." He stood there for a moment, then climbed back into bed.

The clock on the nightstand read 11:32pm and Drew was still awake. The day's events played over and over in his head. He wanted desperately to tell his father about Luke, but his dad seemed a million miles away these days. Disconnected. Drew waited for his parents to come into his room to ground him for his uncharacteristic disrespect at dinner, but the house had grown quiet hours before. *They're slipping*, he thought. He wondered if he'd ever get the opportunity to tell his dad about Luke. Just as he thought he'd give it a rest for the night, he heard a startling noise coming from somewhere within the house. He sat up straining to hear it better. The louder it got, the faster his heart raced. Then he realized, it was that familiar sound of someone crying. He had heard it several times over the last few months. It was the saddest whimper and moan he'd ever heard. It couldn't be the baby crying, he thought. No, this cry was too deep to be Sophia's. Maybe his parents were fighting about him, and his dad made his mom cry. He shook his head, quickly dismissing the thought.

Perhaps there was some truth to what Calvin's brother, Michael, had told him about the old cemetery near the entrance of their neighborhood. He told him that the spirit of the dead wandered through the neighborhood every night looking for its loved ones. If the tale is true, Drew thought, maybe that's what I'm hearing—sad cries from a ghost, because it couldn't find its family. He wanted to get up to make sure everything was okay, but was afraid to. He slowly laid back down, adjusting his pillow to make it more comfortable. The weeping got lower and lower until the house went quiet again. Who was it? What was it? "Mom's right! Maybe I am losing my mind," Drew whispered.

Drew waited and waited for sleep to take over, but how could he sleep? There was too much on his mind. He wasn't supposed to help win that kickball game. He knew he was in trouble with the bully.

He needed help, but from who? Then an unusual and desperate idea came to him. Drew cleared his throat. "Uh, hello God... out there? I've been, uh, praying to you for a while now, maybe since I was about four or so. This might sound crazy... and maybe I'm a little crazy for thinking it. But Sir, if you're real... then I need to schedule a meeting with you. A face-to-face meeting, if that's alright!" Drew waited. There was nothing but silence.

"Hello!" Silence. "I need some help here! I'm pretty sure my dad hates me. Not sure why, but he does. Maybe you can shed some light on the situation. Then I need help with this crazy kid who wants me dead! I haven't done anything to this boy, but he hates my guts. I'm only eleven. Guess if you're real, you already know this. But yeah, it sure would be nice to make it to my twelfth birthday! So, can you help me out, Mr. God? Because if I don't get help from somebody, I might be meeting you real soon anyway!"

He looked around his room for perhaps a sign. Nothing. Only the loud tick tock of the clock on his nightstand. It was 11:58pm. He released most of the wind from his lungs then closed his eyes. What a strange and exhausting day, he thought. He had never felt so alone. The weight of the world seemed to lay heavily on his heart. He turned over onto his stomach then placed the pillow over his head.

CHAPTER THREE

The ride to school the next morning was quiet and awkward. Karen was disappointed in Drew, so she'd said very little even before getting into the car. He knew that he owed his parents an apology, especially his father. He decided to start with her. "Mom, I'm sorry about last night." There was a long pause before he continued. "I'm not sure what got into me. I really don't. But I'm sorry, and it won't ever happen again."

"Son that was quite a display last night! I couldn't figure out if aliens had come and replaced you or not. Are you okay?"

Drew loved his mother so much, but he refused to open up to her about what was bothering him. How could he tell her that the son of whom she was normally so proud is really stupid... a wimp... scum? He thought it would be best for her to focus on Sophia and all the other things that keep moms busy throughout the day.

"I'll be fine."

"Your father loves you a lot, Drew."

Uhmm, I don't think so, but okay, he thought.

"It's just that he's been under a lot of stress lately. But it'll get better soon."

Drew could see her eyes through the rear view mirror, and they even doubted the words that escaped her lips.

"Okay Mom. Thanks." He said what he thought she wanted to hear. Before exiting the car, he leaned over and kissed Sophia's cheek. "Love you baby girl."

"Have a good day, Drew. I love you!"

"Love you too, Mom!"

Drew made his way to his classroom, his eyes scanning his pathway for danger. Would today be the day that Luke unleashed his ultimate fury? Would he pound his face into the ground and cause his parents to not recognize him ever again? He shook his head to remove the thoughts. *No, no, no! Only good things will happen today! Only good things will happen today! Just let him be absent, dear God!*

Only five students got to present their science projects the day before in class 503. As Drew removed items from his backpack, he silently hoped to be one of the students selected today. Ms. Crane had created a lottery system to select students to present their projects. She said it wasn't fair to go in alphabetical order of last name. The students with last names ending in "A" through "E" loved her system.

"Hey Drew, are you nervous about presenting your project? I am!" Anna Fisher sat in the seat in front of Drew's. She always did well on her written work, but she was jittery when it came to public speaking. "I'll give you a million dollars if you present mine for me when she pulls my name!" They both laughed.

"You'll do fine, Anna."

"I hope so."

Although sleepy, Drew was eager to explain the presence of gravity on earth and the absence of the same on the moon. With confidence, he settled into his seat, then opened his homework folder. A yellow envelope sitting in the left pocket caught his eye. How'd that get there? Curiously he reached for it, but hesitated to touch it. What if it was a death threat from Luke, describing in graphic detail how he would kill him? His hands made contact with the letter, sending a strange tingling sensation throughout his body. He shook his head then blinked twice, trying to recover from a sudden dizzy spell. *Stop being a wimp, and just open the letter for crying out loud!* His conscience snapped.

> *Drew,*
>
> *I heard your prayer last night.*
>
> *If you still want to talk, then let's do so tonight.*

I've arranged a special place for our conversation, so be prepared to travel and don't be afraid.

~Your Father

The room started spinning again. Drew had so many thoughts running through his mind, he couldn't keep them straight. One thing was for sure, the note didn't come from Luke. It came from his house. But why would his father stand at his door and listen to his prayers? And of all nights, why last night? Why didn't he just come on in and talk? Drew was embarrassed! He already felt that his father didn't like him. Now he must think his only son is a little off his rocker. "Great!" he mumbled under his breath. Drew looked at the note again, but focused on the last part. *"Be prepared to travel and don't be afraid... "* He frowned. Where does he plan on taking me? To Timbuktu and leaving me? My bedroom would be just fine, Dad!

Drew was distracted in class. His mind kept drifting. He managed, somehow, to give his full attention to his science project when Ms. Crane pulled his name as the first presenter of the day. "Remember, you have only 15 minutes." She reminded her students.

Talking about the moon made Drew happy, providing a needed distraction from the letter. He stood tall and confident, as if bullies didn't exist and all fathers loved their sons unconditionally. "Today class, you will learn facts about the moon and its relationship to planet Earth. Matthew, how old are you?" Drew didn't tell Matthew that he would be called upon during his presentation. With one eyebrow raised, Matthew reluctantly replied, "You know how old I am, Drew. I'm eleven. Eleven year's old!"

"Thank you, Matthew, for being such a great participant. Yes, you are eleven years old, as most of us are in this classroom. I'm sure I would be in big trouble if I asked Ms. Crane her age, so I will refrain." The class burst into muffled giggles, as Ms. Crane gave Drew a guarded smile.

He cleared his throat and continued. "Most of us in class 503 have existed for 11 years, but the moon... the moon has existed for over 4 billion years and it has had an effect on our planet for that amount of time." Drew showed his classmates his models of the moon and earth and captivated them with scientific facts. He explained how the moon's gravity pulls at the earth, effecting the ocean's tides. He shared how the side of the moon that faces the sun is 273 degrees Fahrenheit and that the opposite side is negative 243 degrees. He concluded his presentation by saying, "There are still mysteries about the moon, and in about 15 years or so you will read about me. I'll be that scientist who unravels the mysteries of that great place!" After Drew was done, his classmates were convinced that they too would become astronauts and walk the moon with him one day.

"Well done Andrew!" said Ms. Crane. "Your parents will be proud!"

"Parents..." Hearing Ms. Crane say that word reminded Drew of the letter! He made his way back to his desk, feeling a nervous twitch in his stomach.

"Great job Dr. Carmichael!" Anna whispered, extending her hand for Drew to slap as he passed by.

Ugh... I can't believe he heard me! He shook the thought from his mind. By luck of the draw, Anna's name was pulled next to present her project on dolphins. "Focus, Drew, focus!" he mumbled to himself.

Later that day, Drew informed Ms. Crane that he was having one of those migraine headaches again, and wouldn't be able to play in game #2 of the kickball competition. "Do you need to see the nurse?" she asked as she felt his forehead.

"No, ma'am. She'll just make me lay down, and I'll miss watching the game."

"Well, okay," she said, "but be sure to let me know if it gets worse."

"Yes ma'am, I will."

Truth was, there was no headache. Drew was fine. He just didn't feel like dealing with Luke and his promise of inflicting great pain upon him. So at recess, his classmates ran left towards the field, while he briskly walked straight ahead towards the old oak trees. There were seven in all, but Drew chose the safety of Papa Oak. The tree had been given its' nickname long ago, as it was the oldest and largest on the school yard. Drew kneeled, positioning himself beside the tree and behind the large rectangular stone that kids sometimes used as a chair. It was the perfect spot to view the game and to hide from bullies.

The whistle blew, signaling the start of game two—Ms. Crane's class against Ms. Roosevelt's class. The game got off to a great start, with both teams working hard to score points against the other. Drew was excited to see that it was Matthew's turn to kick. Nelson rolled the ball to him, and Matthew kicked it hard to the far left, sending the opponents scrambling to get it before he made it to 2nd base. Drew suddenly noticed that Luke wasn't one of the ones running to recover the ball. He was missing from the game. Where was he? Drew's eyes darted everywhere, feeling a wave of panic when he couldn't locate him. He saw him at lunch, so Drew knew he was at school. Just as those thoughts entered his mind, Drew felt a strong blow to his lower back that knocked him forward, causing his head to hit the large stone before him. He rolled onto the ground beside the stone.

Luke circled around Drew like an animal would his stunned prey. "Did you think you had a free day from me Drew Carmichael? Huh? Did you really think I'd leave you alone after yesterday? Not a chance! You disgust me! Earth would be a better place without you in it, you pathetic piece of crap!"

Drew leaned against the rock and wiped the dirt from his face. The words that seemed locked inside his mouth for weeks were finally released. "What in the world have I done to you to make you treat me like this? What?"

Startled by Drew's ability to speak, Luke was silent. Drew thought he saw remorse in Luke's eyes. Maybe he was sorry for what he'd been doing. Just like that, it disappeared. His anger returned.

"What did I tell you yesterday, huh? I told you not to play in the game, but you did it anyway. So I'm delivering on my promise Drew-cilla! I'm not going to kill you today, but that day is coming. Believe me, it's coming! Because I don't want you here! I want you dead!"

Drew's lower back throbbed in pain, and he wanted to scream in agony. However, he refused to let Luke see him cry. So he had a private conversation with his tears. *Don't fall right now! Please stay where you are!* He begged. His tears seemed to have pity and obeyed his orders. Drew wiped what he thought was sweat rolling from his forehead, but it was blood streaming from the place his head had struck the rock.

"I don't hurt you, so you have no right to hurt me. You better stop!"

"Or what, huh? Or what scum bag? Your little helper isn't here to help you now. You're on your own." Luke bent down and whispered, "I hate you so much, I curse the ground you walk on."

"But why?" Drew really wanted an answer, as he continued wiping away the blood.

"Just because Drew Carmichael... just because!" Luke laughed. As he taunted Drew, he scanned the area, making sure no one witnessed what was going on.

"You better stop before you get in lots of trouble."

"And how will I get in trouble lab monkey? Huh? You're gonna rat me out? Noooo... you won't do that. You're too afraid that your dying day will come quicker. Yeah, if I were you, I would just dust the dirt out of that nappy hair and move along as if this never happened." He stood on top of the rock and delivered another swift blow to the back of Drew's head, then walked away fast.

Drew picked himself up, slowly dusting dirt from his hair and front side, just as his bully had instructed. Drew looked around. The kickball game was still in progress. Everyone's eyes were glued to the action, including the teachers. "God help me!"

CHAPTER FOUR

The distance between Papa Oak and the nurse's office seemed lands apart for Drew's unsteady legs. The classroom doors along the way seemed to move off their hinges, then back again. The floor leaned sideways causing him to lean to the other side to steady himself. He'd once read in a newspaper article that when souls hurt, the body cries clear tears; but when the body hurts, red tears. He'd already won the battle to keep the clear ones from falling. He pressed hard against his forehead to stop the red tears from oozing. The main hallway smelled of pencil erasers and pinto beans. It was a welcoming aroma, a sign to Drew that he was almost there.

Drew entered the nurse's office and was relieved that no other students were there. He explained to Nurse Mary that he stumbled and hit his head on a rock. His story smelled fishy, but she accepted it. Drew was one of the good kids at Sterling Creek: gifted and talented, well behaved, and athletic. Why would he lie? So she dismissed the patch of dirt and leaves at the back of his head, and the dirt stain on the lower part of his white shirt. She cleaned and dressed his wound with a bandage and allowed him to lay down for 30 minutes to ease the headache. He convinced her that calling his mother was unnecessary, so she wrote a note to send home with him instead. In the note, she advised his mother to have his eyesight evaluated by an ophthalmologist because of his frequent visits to the nurse's office complaining of headaches. The rest of the school day was a blur to Drew, but it was finally the weekend. A two day break from pain. A break from fear.

At dismissal, he made a quick detour to the restroom to pull the bandage off, hoping the bump on his head would be less noticeable to his mother. He had no intention of showing her the nurse's note. He put it in the tiny compartment of his backpack with the other eight nurse's notes. She didn't need to worry, Drew figured.

On the ride home, he thought how relieved he'd be once his father gave him tips on how to protect himself against bullies. He no longer felt embarrassed about the letter. He only wanted to spend time with his dad over pizza. At least that's what he imagined would happen that night. His dad would arrive home at an earlier time from work, take him to Congo's Pizza Parlor, and the two would remain there way past his bed time. After all, this conversation was overdue, especially after today's assault. Drew couldn't wait.

The thought of biting into a warm slice of Congo's pizza took his mind off his aching body.

There were two routes between Sterling Creek Elementary and the Carmichael home. Drew's mom always took the back way on Fridays—kind of a special treat. It was a longer route, but the payoff was sweet. There were less cars and no traffic lights. The route also ran alongside La Paloma Chateaux, a fancy resort and spa, situated on 400 sprawling acres of rolling meadows and majestic trees. Those with deep pockets traveled there for vacations, and the well-to-do locals frequented the place for nice dinners, spa treatments, and leisure horseback riding. Drew loved watching the horses prance beside the white picket fence that enclosed the ranch. Sometimes passers-by could see cowboys training for some special event. Other times, a group of kids could be seen grooming their mare right before riding lessons.

Drew normally enjoyed pointing out the horses to Sophia as they drove by. This time, though, he said nothing.

"Hey, you alright back there? You're pretty quiet."

"I'm okay. Just tired. That's all."

"Did you present your project today?"

"I did. Think I did okay." His tone was flat. Lifeless.

Karen told him how proud she was of him, and hoped he got selected for the district's science fair. Drew didn't respond. He wondered when the weird stars that floated before him would finally go away.

—◯—

They arrived home a few minutes later. Karen unbuckled Sophia who had been lulled to sleep by the car ride.

"Hey Mom, did Dad mention where he was taking me tonight?"

"Drew, close the door for me, please. Thanks."

He did as requested. "So did he?"

"Did who what?" she asked nonchalantly, as they entered the house through the garage door.

"Dad. Did he tell you where he was taking me tonight?"

"I'm sorry son. I have no idea what you're talking about. When did he tell you he was taking you somewhere?" She didn't wait for a response. She walked through the kitchen and carried the baby into the living room, laying her down in the playpen. She then returned.

Drew was puzzled. "Well... "

"If he did, I'm sure he didn't mean today. He's working late tonight. Remember the project he's been working on? Well, maybe you don't. Dad has this major project deadline. He and his team can't leave the office until it's finished." Drew was uninterested in the particulars of the project, but she continued providing detail after detail. He was no longer listening. He sat down at the kitchen table and stared at the daily newspaper he enjoyed reading every day after school. Why would Dad go through the trouble of leaving a note for me if he knew he wouldn't be able to honor it? Why? Drew wondered.

"Son, what's going on with you? Are you okay? And what's wrong with your back?" Drew hadn't realized that he was rubbing one of the areas where Luke assaulted him. He quickly moved his hand away.

"Huh? Oh it's nothing. I'm okay!"

She continued studying him, because something didn't seem right. She moved in closer to examine the knot on his head. "Drew, what happened to you here?"

"Huh? Oh this? Psshhh... Clumsy me! I fell at recess. Bumped my head on a rock. But I'm good though."

"Are you sure child? You don't look like you're good. You have dirt all in your hair. This knot on your forehead! You look a mess! Did you at least go to the nurse?"

"Yes, Mom. I did and I'm fine, okay. But hey, back to Dad. Are you sure he's working late tonight?"

"Drew, I'm 100% positive. Besides, your father never said anything to me about taking you anywhere. Did you dream that?" She chuckled, as she removed snacks from the pantry for Drew. He searched for the humor in her question but found none. The headache and back pain seemed to suddenly intensify. Hearing her response was like Luke delivering another blow in the same areas. He could even hear Luke's taunts! *You idiot! Your father doesn't love you! Heck, he doesn't even like you! He hates you just like I do. Scum-bag!"* He shook his head in dismay.

"Mom, I'm not hungry. It's been a long day. I'm gonna lay down for a bit."

"What? And not read the newspaper?"

"I'll read it later."

"Oh, alright then." She watched him as he reached down to grab his backpack and walked to the stairs. She shook her head, dismissing his appearance and questions as just pre-teen weirdness.

Drew thought about the letter all the way up the stairs. By the time he reached the top, he wondered if he had hallucinated the whole thing. The thought was enough to make him pick up his pace to his room. He threw his backpack on top of the desk and stared at it for a moment. "If there is no letter in this backpack, I'll need to have my head examined!" He pulled his homework folder out and carefully opened it. He breathed a sigh of relief. It was still there. He grabbed the envelope and that familiar tingling sensation returned. This is so weird, he thought. He unfolded it and discovered nothing had changed. The words were the exact same. He scratched his head, causing dirt to fall onto the letter. It proved to be no distraction from his deep thoughts. *"Be prepared to travel and don't be afraid... "*

"It doesn't make sense! Why would I be afraid? Why would I... be afraid?" The clock on Drew's nightstand struck 4:31 pm, and it hit him like a lightning bolt on a stormy day. Drew finally understood. The letter had not been written by his father, Andrew Carmichael, Sr. It had, in fact, been written by... "Our Father, who art in Heaven!" Drew dropped the letter and slowly pushed away from the desk. He started pacing the floor. "Oh my God!" With both his hands cradling his soiled head, he repeated those three words over and over again. "Oh my God! Oh my God! Oh my God!"

He peered out the window to make sure he didn't see monkeys riding on bikes on the sidewalk. That certainly would prove that he was no longer playing with a full deck... crazy! But what he saw was normal activity. Twins Caleb and Cory were skate-boarding across the street, and Mr. Emmerson was passing by with his dog, Scout, on their normal afternoon stroll. Somewhat relieved, he stumbled to the other side of the room to retreat into his dark closet. He leaned against the left interior wall, then slid down into a crouching position. He had to get a grip on his thoughts. "Did God write this note to me?" he asked aloud. He returned to his desk and slowly reached for the letter. When the tips of his trembling fingers touched it again, a surge of adrenalin coursed stronger through his body. Tears clouded his vision. "You heard me! You really heard me!"

The feeling was indescribable! It must've been the way Nana felt when she had a sign that God was real. When Drew spent a month in South Carolina with his grandparents the summer before, he and Nana would oftentimes sit under the tall oak tree in the backyard. They would eat sweet watermelon and talk about whatever came to mind: school, current events, and many times about God. Drew recalled the conversation that gave him chill bumps one hot and steamy afternoon. "So Nana, tell me. How do you know that God is real?"

"Well grandson, I can't answer that question in just one sentence, but I think you might find my explanation interesting! You know, my mama and daddy took us kids to church every Sunday when I was just a girl. It didn't matter how hot or how cold it was. We were at Sunday school at 9:30am sharp!" She laughed at the memory. "We learned just about everything in the bible: how God created our world, about the first man and woman, and certainly about God's son, Jesus. So as a child, I believed everything we learned and loved worshipping God most times when we went to church. I couldn't see Him, baby, but I sure could feel Him. But you know, when I got to be 17 or 18, I started to rebel 'cause I got tired of being at church all the time like Mama and Daddy. So I convinced myself that church was for weak people and that God was just a fairy tale they made up. Mama and Daddy were so disappointed, Drew, but they let me figure things out on my own, you know. So I stopped praying and if I went to church, it was only to make my parents feel good. I would just sit there, but my mind would be on other things like boys!" She laughed. "Very soon, I stopped feeling His Spirit. I felt empty inside. I was having fun out there, but I'd always go home still feeling like something was missing in my life. One night, I remember going home from a party and just feeling so down. You know, sad and empty. I got ready for bed and just laid there, staring up at the ceiling. Then suddenly I heard myself say, 'God, I think I miss You, and I'm not even sure why. If you are real, forgive me for walking away from Your love. In my heart, I wanna believe You're real, but I have my doubts. Can you just show your child a sign, please? If You do, then I will worship You for the rest of my days.'

"So what happened?" Drew was curious.

"Well, that night I fell asleep! Had partied too much!" She laughed.

"But the next day was Saturday. Mama and Daddy had invited some friends over for a small backyard barbeque. My Godparents, Doris and Leroy, were there. Leroy had just bought a new Polaroid camera, and he was snapping pictures of everybody and everything. Just having fun and showing off all at the same time!"

"Uh, what's a Polar camera?"

She laughed at her grandson. "It's called Polaroid. It was an instant camera. You pushed the button at the top, and the picture would slide right out the other end, just like that! But, we had to wait a minute or two for the picture to develop. Then we'd peel off this protective cover to reveal the picture. We thought it was pretty fancy at the time, but nowadays everything is digital this, digital that. Anyway, we had a good ole time eating, laughing, and dancing. After a while, we noticed a big storm cloud in the distance, and it looked like it was heading our way. The weatherman mentioned a possible storm, but nobody believed him. Well, he was right this time. So we started packing things up and taking them into the house. While we were busy doing that, Leroy snapped a picture of that scary looking cloud. Daddy told him he would get struck by lightning if he didn't put that camera away. He just laughed. When the picture came out of the camera, he gave it to me to hold until it was time to peel the cover off. Then he decided he'd help take in the last chairs. So after a little bit, I peeled the covering off the picture... and what I saw Andrew Carmichael took my breath away!"

Drew had been laying on his side, propped up by his left arm. However, he sat straight up to hear the rest of the story. Nana's voice had started to shake and her eyes watered.

"I can't ever tell this story without crying." She hesitated for a moment, then continued. "The picture was indeed of that black cloud, but that wasn't the only thing that Leroy captured. High in the sky, in the center of that cloud was the image of a man. He wore a white robe and a rope tied around his waist. He had his arms extended outward, as if he was welcoming people unto him. I believe it was God. No! I know it was God!"

"Really, Nana? What did He look like?"

"Funny thing, Drew, is that black cloud covered his face... almost on purpose. My hands trembled while I held that picture and I couldn't stop the tears from flowing—kinda like now." She laughed while Drew waited anxiously to hear more. "Mama saw me crying and rushed over to see what was wrong. I couldn't speak. I just handed her the picture. She studied it briefly, then she covered her mouth to keep from screaming or something. Everyone came over to see what was going on. That picture went from hand to hand, and everyone was shocked beyond belief. Leroy studied it for a while, then he handed it back to me. When I grabbed the tip of the picture again, a surge of energy rushed through my body, and no longer could I hold back the tears. I cried out loud, because God was speaking to me. He had answered my prayers. That picture was a visible sign that He was real. Grandson, those who seek Him will find Him. It may not always be in the same way, but He always answers. So from that point on, I never questioned whether God was real or not. And trust me child, I have gone through some very tough things in my life—things that would cause the strongest Christian to be angry and walk away from God. But I refuse to walk away. I would rather have Him in my life while I go through a storm than to walk away from Him because of one. In the bible, God never promised us that life would be easy, but He did promise to always be with us. And now, I would have it no other way." She paused. "One day, I pray that you fully understand what I mean. Go in the house and get Nana some tissue. You got me out here crying and carrying on!" She laughed and swatted at him. Drew left and returned quickly, handing her the tissue.

"So Nana, where is that picture? Did the Leroy guy let you keep it?"

"Only for a couple weeks, then he came back for it. I never saw it again. No one knows what Leroy did with that picture. Some say he sold it, but no one

really knows. It didn't matter to me. That picture will
be etched in my memory forever."

Drew got chill bumps remembering that conversation.
He wished Nana could be with him right then to meet
God in person. Then of course, if God never showed
up, proving that Drew was really losing his mind,
she'd be there to comfort him as only a grandmother
could. He wondered what time he would be picked up.
Would God just walk up to his front door and ring
the doorbell? What would his mother think? Would
she call the police or pass flat out? "Will I pass out?"
Drew said aloud. He laughed to himself. *I hope I'm
not losing my mind! Should I shower and brush my
teeth?*

The wind started to pick up outside, causing the
leaves to pull away from their branches and scatter
about. The temperature dropped from a comfortable
81 degrees to a chilly 43 degrees. The sun exited
left allowing the moon and the stars to take center
stage. The stars twinkled against the dark sky, and
the moon... well, it's perfectly round and orange face
commanded the attention of every individual who
happened to be outside. It hung so low, it appeared to
be sitting on the edge of earth, as if it had come down
to kiss earth good night. Perhaps it knew something
extraordinary was about to happen.

Chapter Five

Drew was oblivious to the night's beauty outside his window. He was too busy trying to keep calm, hoping that he wasn't losing his mind. Maybe the damaged cells from his injuries had taken up residence in his brain, causing all the weird and abnormal thoughts. However, just in case this was real, he chose to roll with it. His room was now dark with just a hint of illumination from the moon. His heart finally beat at a normal pace, but he watched the clock on his nightstand change minute by minute. The clock struck 6:49 when he heard a calm deep voice say to him, "Hello Drew. It is time."

Drew jumped straight up from his bed as if a blaring fire alarm had gone off. He frantically looked around for the source of the voice. His heart started to beat out of control again. He saw no one. The voice spoke again. "Do you remember the last thing I wrote to you, Drew?"

Of course he knew. He'd rehearsed the note over and over in his mind, remembering every single word. His mouth was dry, but he somehow found his voice. "You said... you said for me to not be afraid."

"That's right, my child. There is no need to be afraid. Calm your mind and your spirit." Drew didn't fully comprehend the statement, but he understood enough to close his eyes and take deep breaths to slow the pace of his heart. There was something about this voice that assured Drew that he was safe and that everything was going to be okay.

"That's good, my son. That's good!" The voice said.

Drew fumbled with the lamp, eventually turning it on so he could better scan the room for the source of the voice. He saw no one.

"Where are you? I... I thought you would ring the doorbell and... and meet my mom and all."

"I am everywhere, Drew. But you won't see me here; only at our meeting place. I believe we have lots to talk about, so you should start your journey now. Go to your window."

My window? Stranger danger crossed Drew's mind. "This might be a dumb question... "

"No question is dumb," the voice quickly replied.

"Uh, okay. Well, I need to be sure who you are before... before I do what you are telling me to do. Who are you?"

The voice chuckled softly. "I am the One who you pray to every night. The Creator of the universe and of mankind. I am God."

"Okay, Okay... I was just checking! Okay, I'm coming." Drew's feet were like heavy bricks treading through knee-deep water, as he walked obediently to the window. His head seemed to hurt worse. He wasn't sure his mind was ready to see what was on the other side, so he closed his eyes and slowly drew back the curtain. What he saw when he opened his eyes took his breath away. "You have got to be kidding me!" He slapped himself hard to make sure he wasn't dreaming.

At the edge of his window was a staircase made of Mahogany. It started at the base of his window and extended all the way to that place Drew had dreamed of visiting, the moon. His mouth fell wide open. God chuckled.

"Sir, the meeting... is going to be up there... on the moon?"

"Would you prefer a different place, such as Congo's?"

"Oh, no sir! No sir! The moon pleases me just fine! It really does! Oh My God!"

God raised the window, and instructed Drew to climb onto the staircase. Drew took his first step onto the stairs and jumped up and down. The stairs did not shake or sway. He smiled. Of all the newspaper articles he'd ever read regarding paranormal activity, none had ever spoken of what he was experiencing. He looked up and wondered how many steps he would have to take to finally arrive at his destination. There must be over a billion steps, he thought. Then he heard the voice say, "Don't be concerned with how many steps there are. Just start your journey and you'll arrive at the appointed time."

"What if I get tired, and don't make it?"

"You'll make it, my son! Just one step at a time."

With that affirmation, Drew took his second step... then his third... and his fourth. Eager to make it to his destination, he started running by leaps and bounds, ignoring his aches and pains. The voice was silent, but Drew continued in confidence. After a short while, he paused to see how far he'd climbed. The moon's light shined upon everything, allowing him to easily see the homes in his neighborhood. They appeared as toy fixtures. He looked to the far right of his neighborhood in search of the tallest building in downtown Solome. It was where his father worked. He found it and noticed several office lights still on. He was saddened. He works late so he doesn't have to come home, he thought. He turned toward the meeting place, the topic of his science project, and the place he hoped to get answers and help. It looked grand. Majestic! Unreal!

As he continued his climb, a million thoughts ran through his mind. He wondered what God would look like and how the moon would feel under his feet. Then he noticed that the wind wasn't blowing nor was it raining or snowing. The temperature was perfect. He wasn't tired or thirsty, a huge difference from when he played kickball at recess and ran laps at P.E. All these things racing through his mind overwhelmed him as none of what was happening made sense.

None at all. Yet somehow, he knew it was real and he knew he needed to follow through. Besides, the meeting was what he had asked for.

It wasn't long before Drew effortlessly passed through Earth's atmosphere and into outer space. He knew that, under normal circumstances, this action was impossible to accomplish without the protection of a man-made spaceship equipped with all of the necessities of human life, like air. The One who was granting this meeting was still silent, but Drew knew He was with him, protecting him. He could feel His presence. As he drew nearer, the perimeter of the moon could no longer be seen and Earth had become like a shiny marble, appearing as perfect as the day its Creator formed it in the palm of His hands.

Then, finally, there were only seven steps left to take between him and the meeting place. Instead of leaping forward as fast as he could, Drew stood still. He tilted his head backward and closed his eyes, preparing to embrace what was to come. *Why does He care so much, that He would arrange all of this for me?* Drew pondered. His heart swelled with gratitude. As he prepared to take those final steps, he heard the voice say, "Andrew Carmichael, Jr., come forward!" Drew opened his eyes to finally behold this Stranger his grandparents had taught him to pray to.

As Drew took those last steps toward God, he felt totally unnecessary—like he and his problems, in comparison to the grandeur of the Almighty, were simply nothing! Yet somehow he knew that he mattered. He stepped from the staircase onto the moon. Feeling unworthy to stand in God's presence, he collapsed to his knees, instinctively laying his forehead on God's feet. It was a moment when perfection connected with imperfection, causing that familiar surge of energy to course through his body again. God laid His right hand on the crown of Drew's head and his back pain suddenly vanished. The headache and the knot that caused it disappeared. Drew felt like a brand new eleven year old. He looked up at God with trembling lips and whispered, "Thank You!"

"You are welcome, my child."

God grabbed both Drew's hands, helping him to stand. "Follow Me. I knew you'd be hungry when you arrived, so I thought we'd start with dinner."

Wait, how did He know... ? Drew interrupted his own thought. He is God. He knows everything! Drew smiled. He figured that if God knew he was hungry, then He also knew what he wanted to talk about. He could hardly wait.

There was a large pizza box sitting on a boulder and beside that boulder were two smaller rocks that appeared smooth enough on top to comfortably sit. Drew knew that God had arranged that as well. "Have a seat." He sat as instructed and quickly recognized that the pizza was from his favorite pizza parlor, Congo's. Drew scratched his head in confusion, then he thought, *I won't even ask!*

He put his hands together to bless his food, then realized that the One he had prayed to all these years was now sitting across from him. Drew didn't know what to do. It would be awkward if he did it the way he normally did at home. So he glanced up at God and said, "Thank you so much for this food that I'm about to eat and thank you for selecting my favorite restaurant. In your son Jesus' name I pray. Amen." God looked at Drew like a proud father would his son. "Please, eat."

Drew opened the box and discovered his favorite pizza inside, pepperoni with mushrooms. He was having a-beside-himself moment. *I'm having pizza, on the moon... with God! What a miracle!* He thought. While he ate, he stole a few glances at God, but quickly looked away each time. He was too overcome by the swirl of emotions that birthed fluttering butterflies in the pit of his stomach. He decided to just look down as he finished his meal. When he was done, God handed him a clear container of water to drink. Tasting better than any water he'd ever had, he gulped it down. Then Drew recognized that God had not eaten. He concluded that, perhaps, He never needed to. How cool, he thought.

Drew forced himself to look at God again. "That was delicious! Thank you again." God nodded, but didn't utter a word. He was taller and bigger than any man Drew had ever seen. A gentle giant. His skin was copper toned, and the thick course hair on his head was pure white. His eyes were the color of the clearest island water. He wore a long off-white robe with a thick tan rope tied about His waist. When He spoke, His deep voice reminded Drew of relaxing ocean waves mixed with thunder on a stormy day. The Creator of all, the One who many prayed to, had agreed to meet me, Drew thought. He lowered his head again, feeling unworthy of looking directly at Him. Then God spoke.

"It is okay to look at Me, Drew." He hesitated, but did as he was told. He cleared his throat.

"Thank You for meeting me. I never imagined in my wildest dreams that this could or would ever happen. You know, You meeting me. Then... " Drew felt a plum-sized lump in his throat as he looked around. "Then you chose here—a place you must've known I love so much. You really do exist, just like my Nana and Grandpa said."

"I do." God affirmed.

Drew thought about his mother and father.

"I love them too." God uttered.

"Who, my parents?"

"Yes, of course I do."

"They mean a lot to me, my parents." He cleared his throat again. "But they are so hard to understand, especially my dad."

God smiled again. "Come! Before you tell me what's on your mind, let's take a stroll."

Drew stood up and looked all around. He and God were the only two on the entire moon. "Wow! So you changed the moon's natural climate so I could survive this visit, huh."

"How do you know this to be true?" God quizzed.

"Well for one, there is normally no air on the moon. So I wouldn't be able to breathe without a special mask and astronaut suit. Then two, the temperature here would either fry me or freeze me solid in an instant!" Drew could tell God more cool facts about the moon, except He already knew.

"You've learned a lot about this place."

"I have. I think your work is awesome!"

"Thank you. I think so too."

As they strolled, God gave an eager Drew the grand tour of the moon, allowing him to float and flip like he'd seen the astronaut's weightless bodies do. Then God offered to him information scientists had yet to figure out.

"So God, why didn't you make the moon and the planets a safe place for humans to travel to or even live?" God chuckled.

"Drew, I only intended for man-kind to live on Earth. That's why I created a world so large and so magnificent, you would never grow bored of exploring it. As a matter of fact, there still remain treasures on Earth that have yet to be discovered.

"Wow!"

After a short while, they approached a cliff. It was no ordinary cliff, but nor was this meeting. Drew walked ever so carefully to the edge so that his eyes could take in more. Beyond the cliff was what could be described as the grand canyon of the moon. It was breathtaking geological wizardry. What a wonder, Drew thought, as he stood there with his mouth slightly open in disbelief. Noticing how steep the drop was, he instinctively jumped backward.

"Let's sit here for a while Drew." God sat on the very edge of the cliff, allowing his long legs to dangle over the 7,000 foot cliff. Drew hesitated. He didn't particularly like dangling his feet over 3 feet of water at the neighborhood pool, for fear of being pushed in by the likes of Luke. So he couldn't imagine dangling his feet over a cliff. However, Luke was far from the moon and Drew figured this was the absolute safest place in the universe to be, in the company of God Almighty. He acquiesced, but sat very close to Him. The Creator and His child both sat looking ahead.

CHAPTER SIX

E xploring the moon had been nothing less than epic to Drew. As they sat, he pinched himself, making sure he wasn't dreaming.

"Now, Drew. This would be a good time to discuss why you requested this meeting." Drew looked up at Him, but God continued gazing forward. He appeared serious. Business-like. Drew felt tiny sitting beside Him. He glanced down at his hands that fiddled nervously in his lap.

"Nana said that You know all things. Is that true?" Drew asked timidly.

"I do."

"So, then you already know my troubles."

"Drew, I desire that you to talk to Me as if I don't already know what is bothering you."

"But why?"

"Because it is what I require of you, when you pray or talk to Me. It strengthens your relationship with Me." Drew scratched his head. *We're in a relationship?*

"If you were home and you wanted to talk to Me, how would you do that?" God asked.

"I guess I would have to pray to You."

"Did I already know what you would pray?"

"Yes, I suppose so."

"Then why did you continue to pray, if I already knew?"

Drew pondered his question for a moment. "Hmmm... Well, here's the truth. Nana said I had to!" He giggled. "But I must say, God, that when I did pray, I felt like someone heard me; like I was connected to something. Is that the relationship that made me feel close to you?"

"Yes, my child, it was. Always remember, there can be no true relationship without communication. I designed mankind to yearn for relationship and what makes that relationship strong is communication. So again... " With His deep commanding voice, God said, "Tell Me why you called this meeting."

Drew bowed his head again, feeling somewhat afraid to tattle on his bully. He could hear Luke saying, "If you tell someone, I'll kill you." His heart beat wildly. "There's this kid at my school. His name is Luke." He paused, then found his voice again. "I'm scared of him because... well, he hurts me." Drew admired the stars, as they performed for their Creator and His guest. They calmed him as he continued.

"He punches me in the stomach. He kicks me from behind and trips me. He spits on me so much, I have to carry Kleenex in my back pocket to wipe it off. And last week, when I was leaving the boy's restroom, he was walking in. When I tried passing him, he just stepped in my way. I knew he was about to do something to me, so I started backing up. Then he just grabbed me by my neck with both his hands and pushed me against the wall. I tried to get away, but the more I pushed, the more pressure he put on my neck. I couldn't breathe. Then right before I passed out, he swung me to the floor and walked out. He didn't even use the restroom." Drew shook his head. "I'm afraid of what he'll do next. Whatever it is, if it doesn't kill me, it'll surely make me cry. And I don't wanna cry in front of him."

"Why not?" God's voice seemed to echo throughout the canyon. As Drew pondered the question, a bright asteroid suddenly passed over the canyon and exploded a safe distance away.

"Whoa, that was awesome!"

"Nice fireworks, huh!" They both laughed. "Continue", God said.

"I have absolutely no idea what I was about to say!"

"You said you didn't want to cry in front of Luke. Why Not?"

"Oh right!" His tone became solemn again. "Well, it's all I have left. If he sees me crying, then he wins the battle, or worse. He may think it's a signal to hurt me more, maybe even finish me off. I don't know. I'm not sure I am even making sense."

"I understand you, My child." God smiled.

"Okay, good! I just want it to stop, but I don't know how." He paused, then continued. "That leads me to my other problem—my father. I've tried to talk to him so many times about Luke, but... " He stalled.

"But what?"

"He won't talk to me. My mom says that his stressful job tires him out before he gets home."

"Do you believe that?"

"Not really! I know his job might be super hectic, but so is Mr. Jacob's job. He runs a real big company with lots of employees, but he still finds time to take Matthew to baseball games and to monster truck events. You know, father-son stuff." Drew stared beyond the moon's canyon, resting his eyes on nothing in particular. He was finding it easier to tell God all his worries. "I think it's me."

"Oh?"

"I do. Something tells me that my dad doesn't like me anymore. When he looks at me, he looks angry... sometimes even sad or disappointed. I have no idea what I've done to him. He won't tell me."

"Well, have you asked him?"

"I've tried to talk to him, but he doesn't say much back."

"Drew, did you specifically ask him if he was angry or disappointed with you? Did you ask him if he hated you or was embarrassed of you?"

"No. I haven't."

"Then it is not fair to your father to believe those things. Don't expect answers if you do not ask for them! Don't expect change if you do nothing to make it happen."

"Well, do you know why he acts the way he does towards me?"

"I know all things, remember?" God spoke calmly. Drew was frustrated, but comfortable speaking to someone he felt he'd known for a long time. "Drew, if you were struggling to carry a bag almost twice your size, would you be able to help Matthew carry his bag if you saw him having difficulty?"

"I don't think so. I wouldn't be able to carry my heavy bag and his too."

"How, then, do you think you would be able to help him?"

"Well, I guess if I laid my bag down or somehow got rid of it."

"Good answer. So when parents are struggling with their own problems or baggage, they have a difficult time recognizing that their children need help with their baggage too. Your father is having a tough time

with his bag right now, but things will get better soon
and the two of you will be just fine."

"Will You tell me what's in my dad's bag?" Drew was
choked up.

"It'll be revealed to you in time. But until then, just
know that your father loves you more than life itself!"
Drew was glad to hear those words. A weight seemed
to be lifted.

"So back to Luke. Why does he hate me so much?"

"Luke doesn't hate you, Drew."

Drew turned his head real fast toward God, his mouth
open in disbelief. He wanted to tell God that He was
wrong, but quickly dismissed the thought.

"Well, how can that be? He certainly doesn't hurt me
because he loves me!"

The two sat in silence. Drew was desperate for a
response, but God offered none. After what seemed
like forever to Drew, God spoke. "I'm going to give
you a glimpse of what goes on in a home not very far
from your own." God stretched out his right arm and
a gigantic theater-sized screen suddenly appeared
over the canyon, right before the two of them. The
performing stars moved away, and the area was
darkened. This was becoming more unbelievable to
Drew. A movie on the moon with God? How exciting,
he thought. But as the images appeared on the
screen, his smile disappeared. Goose-bumps formed
the length of his arms, and his heart beat at a rapid
pace. It became very clear that this was no movie for

entertainment. It was activity inside the home of his bully.

"Can I hug her?" Luke asked.

"Do not put your filthy hands on her! She doesn't even know you're here anyway. And if she did, she wouldn't want a germ like you touching her. You're the reason she's dying. Matter of fact, get out of here. I don't wanna breathe the same air you're breathing."

"Please Phil, just let me spend a little more time with her." The man grabbed the back of Luke's collar and lifted him up from the chair he was sitting.

"When I give you an order, you do it!" The man released Luke's collar. He lifted his right foot and kicked Luke in the back so hard, his body flew through the bedroom door onto the hallway floor. He then walked over and kicked the back of Luke's head with his foot. Luke knew that if he tried to get up, Phil would just knock him down again. So he laid there, hoping for Phil to walk away, slamming the bedroom door behind him. However, the door didn't shut. It only meant one thing. Phil wasn't done. Phil kneeled beside Luke and whispered in his right ear. "She would rather die than be your mother. She hates you that much!"

"That's not true Phil!"

"Shut it up! It is true. She hates you! I hate you and so does your no-good father! That's why he left a long time ago." Phil's breath wreaked of alcohol, so Luke decided to breathe through his mouth so he didn't have to endure the odor. "That's why he doesn't call or visit you. No one wants a stupid kid around, especially me! So when your mother finally kicks the bucket, you won't be my problem anymore. I plan to send you far away; that's if I don't kill you first!" He was silent for a moment, then continued with a laugh. "Yeah, it won't be long before you have another address. Then I can clean... clean out this house and start over like... like you never existed. Get up you... you disgusting lab monkey!"

Luke tried to get up as fast as he could, but he couldn't escape the spit that landed on his neck. He slowly walked down the hall, trying to ignore that familiar pain he'd felt so many times over the last 4 years of his life. It wasn't just his back that hurt; his heart did too.

After a long overdue shower, Luke tip-toed into the kitchen to find food. He heard a sound that was music to his ears—snoring. Phil was fast asleep in the lazy-boy chair in the living room. Hearing him snore made Luke feel safe, because he knew Phil wouldn't rise again until the home health nurse returned the next morning to care for his mom. He quickly made himself a cold bologna sandwich and grabbed a bag of chips from the pantry.

He felt grateful for the next door neighbors, Mr. and Mrs. Cantu. If it weren't for them, there wouldn't be much food to eat. Phil went to work during the day, and would come straight home to relieve the nurse. Afterward, he would get drunk. The Cantus knew that Luke's mom was ill, and they rarely saw Phil bringing bags of food home. So they regularly brought food to their home to help out. He shoved the last piece of sandwich into his mouth, then walked slowly past Phil and carefully to his mother's room.

The bedside lamp provided the right amount of lighting, casting a soft glow onto her face. Luke sat in the chair beside the bed, and held her pale hand. She looked frail and tired to him. Only strands remained of her once thick blonde hair. He longed to see her blue eyes and her bright smile again, but she hadn't been awake for weeks. He leaned over and whispered in her ear, "Hi Mom, it's me Luke. I'm sorry that you're so sick. If I am the reason, like Phil says, then I am so sorry. Can you just try and get better for me? Please! Stay a little while longer, maybe 40 more years or so. Don't leave me here with him. I want you to stay!" He kissed her hand and rested his head beside hers. Tears fell from Luke's eyes. The scene faded away.

Drew looked at God, his eyes searching for answers.

"Keep watching Drew."

There's more? Drew thought. His eyes reluctantly returned to the big screen.

It was so quiet in room 502, you could hear a pen drop. With folded arms, Ms. Roosevelt walked from row to row, overseeing her students as they took their timed math quiz. Based on their facial expressions, most of them appeared confident about their answers. Ms.

Roosevelt walked to the last row and to the last seat where Luke sat. She noticed him tapping his pencil onto his test paper while he stared out the window.

"Have you completed your test Luke?"

"Uh, no ma'am!"

"Well, I suggest you focus. You have only five more minutes before the test is over."

Luke looked at his paper. He had only attempted the first question. He knew he wouldn't complete the test, nor did he care. Besides, there was no one at home to make proud. No one. His mom was unresponsive and his stepdad hated him. He twirled his pencil as Phil's voice repeated all the mean things he'd said to him. "You're so stupid, you will probably flunk 5th grade. They don't let dummies go on to 6th grade. You're so dumb, you'll never make it to high school."

It was 2 minutes left in the test, and Luke's mind recalled the last beating he'd received from Phil. He snapped his pencil in two. Then the buzzer sounded.

"Times up! Put your pencils down and turn your papers over!" Ms. Roosevelt waited for all the students to follow her instructions, then asked them to pass their papers to the front of their row. After all the tests had been collected, the students lined up to head outside for recess. They were hoping to win at least one game against Ms. Crane's class.

Luke's face was red with anger as he exited the building and scanned the yard for someone in particular. Ms. Crane's class had not come out yet, so he waited. The longer he waited, the more furious he became. He thought about how Phil would periodically shut the water valve off outside, forcing him to go to school without a shower. His hands instinctively balled into fists. Seconds later, he saw Annie and the rest of class 503 running onto the field. The one that Luke looked for was the last to come out, and he appeared frightened. Luke watched him, as he walked cautiously to the big oak tree. Finally, this person of interest bent down beside the tree and started watching classes 502 and 503 prepare to battle it out in game two of the kickball competition. Luke waited a moment, then started walking toward the tree, being careful not to be seen. His heart pounded hard against his chest as he got closer and closer. When he was directly behind the unsuspecting crouching boy, he stood quietly and waited. Just as Matthew kicked the ball, and the cheering became a thunderous roar, Luke took three steps back and then rushed forward delivering a strong kick to the boy's lower back. While he was down, he stomped the boy's back hard as if his own life depended on it.

Luke circled his victim.

"Did you think you had a free day from me Drew Carmichael? Huh! Did you really think I'd leave you alone after yesterday? Not a chance! You disgust me! Earth would be a better place without you in it!"

The boy picked himself up, and wiped the dirt from his face. "What in the world have I done to you to make you treat me like this? What?"

"What did I tell you yesterday, huh? I told you not to play in the game, but you did it anyway. So I'm delivering on my promise Drew-cilla! I'm not going to kill you today, but that day is coming. Believe me, it's coming. Because I don't want you here! I want you dead!"

The boy appeared to be in pain. "I don't hurt you, so you have no right to hurt me. You better stop!" Blood streamed from his forehead.

"Or what, huh? Or what scum bag? Your little helper isn't here to help you now. You're on your own." Luke bent down and whispered, "I hate you so much, I curse the ground you walk on."

"But why?"

"Just because Drew Carmichael. Just because!"

"You better stop before you get in lots of trouble", the boy said.

"And how will I get in trouble Drew-cilla? Huh? You're gonna rat me out? Noooo... you won't do that. You're too afraid that your dying day will come quicker. Yeah, if I were you, I would just dust the dirt out of that nappy hair, and move along as if this never happened." He delivered another swift blow to the back of the boy's head, then walked away.

Luke left the boy, and walked toward Ms. Roosevelt. "May I go inside to use the restroom?"

"That's fine. Make sure to come right back."

"Yes ma'am. I will." Luke ran into the building and walked briskly into the boy's restroom. He walked into the last stall and slid the latch closed. He leaned against the door and the tears began to fall.

"What are you doing?" He screamed at himself. "You can't be like him! You can't! So stop it Luke! Stop hurting people you idiot! Just stop it!" He slapped himself over and over again.

The scene faded away, and the screen disappeared.

God and Drew sat in silence once more. Drew was shocked and a little disturbed. He wondered why he suddenly cared, and why he felt such a profound sadness for his bully.

"God?" It was all he could say.

"I'm listening." God knew he was struggling to find words, so He spoke.

"I know this was hard for you to watch Drew, but I wanted you to see just a glimpse of Luke's life at home. What you witnessed was mild compared to other nights—broken bones, burns, you name it."

"Who is the mean guy? Is it Luke's stepdad?" He was surprised at himself for being concerned.

"Yes."

"What's wrong with his mom? Did Luke poison her or something?"

"Not at all Drew. She is dying from a disease."

"Wow! This is probably the saddest thing I've ever seen." Drew looked up at God. "Can you fix her?"

"She is being fixed, Drew. Just not the way many would want her fixed." He stared into the distance. "It won't be long before her spirit departs her body. She will then go to a special place that I've prepared. There's no suffering there." Drew looked into the direction that God looked. Far beyond the moon was a bright light. It must be Heaven, Drew thought.

"Well, will you please help Luke too?" Then he quickly added, "Just not in the way you're helping his mom. Seems like he really needs You."

God smiled. "I'm proud of you, my son."

"Proud of me? Why?" Drew was confused.

"You just prayed for Me to help your enemy, instead of asking that I help you."

Drew sat slouched, unable to shake the heavy sadness. He couldn't recall a time in his life, besides the bullying episodes, when he'd ever felt so sad. He didn't try to hide how he felt. Besides, there was no need to pretend; God knew.

"And by the way... " God interrupted his thoughts. "The next time you see Luke, don't be afraid. He won't hurt you again."

"Are you sure?" Drew quickly cupped his mouth with his hand. "Please scratch that question. I wasn't thinking!" God winked at him.

"He won't hurt you again. Things will get better, but with your help." Before Drew could ask Him what He meant, God stood, signaling that it was time to move on to something different. "Drew, there is someone I'd like for you to meet." God was looking into the distance again, past the moon's canyon and far beyond the celestial bodies that danced and twinkled nonstop. He stretched out his hand toward Drew. "Come Forth."

Drew stood quickly and grabbed God's hand. To his delight, they lifted and floated away from the moon towards the place that appeared very bright. Drew wanted to ask God about this someone, but the question became irrelevant when they both went airborne. This kind of thing didn't happen all the time, Drew thought, unless one was strapped tight in the seat of a theme park ride. "This is unbelievable!" It was all he could think to say. He decided to take in the adventure in silence. He'd find out soon enough who this person was.

CHAPTER SEVEN

Moments later, they arrived to a place that appeared much like earth, except it wasn't. It couldn't be, Drew thought, because the atmosphere felt different. The seemingly endless field was blanketed with a mixture of tall green grass and vibrant wildflowers. Beyond the daisies, asters, and purple shooting stars were varying types of massive trees that stretched taller and wider than any Drew had ever seen. The breeze was fragrant, reminding him of the times he spent at Nana and Grandpa's house. Except it wasn't scorching hot. It was simply perfect here.

Then seemingly out of nowhere, a girl that looked about Drew's age emerged from where the trees stood, and began skipping through the field towards them. She was laughing and yelling something that wasn't clear. Is this who God wants me to meet? Drew wondered.

"I... ing ah ah! I... ming... ah ah!" She said, then burst into giggles. Drew strained to hear her better, but she was still too far away. After a while, he understood every word. "I'm coming Abba... I'm coming!!! I'm coming Abba... I'm coming!" Drew assumed she was talking to God, because when he looked up at Him, He winked and returned his glance towards the girl.

"She's a 12 year old ball of energy, so get ready!" God kept His eyes on her and so did Drew. When she was only a few feet away, God extended his arms toward her and she skipped right into his embrace.

"Abba!"

"Hello my angel!" God hugged her tight like a father would his daughter. Drew watched this interaction, and was overcome by a strong sense that he already knew this caramel-colored girl. When God released her, Drew instinctively hugged her too. Then to his own surprise, he picked her up and turned her around! She laughed hysterically. Startled by his own behavior, Drew landed her safely to the ground.

"I am so so sorry! Forgive me. I don't know what made me do that!"

"Don't apologize! I loved it!" She playfully curtsied. "I'm Carrie."

"Uh, hi Carrie. I'm Drew. Well, it's really Andrew, but everyone calls me Drew for short."

"I know who you are!" She proclaimed. Drew was taken aback by her response, but before he could inquire, Carrie bolted off into the field again. She yelled back to him. "Come with me, Drew. I wanna show you something." Drew looked back at God. "Is it okay? I mean, do we have time? Wait, who is she, and why did I just... " God interrupted him with a deep chuckle.

"Time doesn't exist right now, my child. So Go! Have fun!" He gave Drew an encouraging nudge.

Drew ran as fast as he could to catch up to her—this girl he'd never met, but just gave the warmest embrace. Carrie eventually slowed down so that Drew could catch up. When he did, she grabbed his hand and led the way. She seemed eager to show him something. As they walked, Drew looked all around. This place felt amazing to him. Dad would die to have grass this green, Drew thought. He looked ahead at the giant trees. There were too many to count, but Carrie took him to one in particular. They looked tiny as they stood at the base of it.

"Look up!" she said.

There were countless butterflies of all kinds fluttering high above their heads. Drew looked at Carrie who seemed to be in Heaven as she admired them. She held her hand out and a shimmery blue and black one landed on her finger. "Isn't she magnificent Drew? There are thousands here just like her, but from different species. She is a Blue Morph from the Nymphalidae family." After admiring the butterfly for a moment, Carrie motioned her hand into the air. "He created all of this for us."

Drew wondered who she was referring to, until she stole a glance back at God. He felt silly, as if he should've known.

"I was so ecstatic the day I found her! Her wings beckoned me and I couldn't resist." She chuckled. "Beanie told me not to climb so high to reach her, but you know me... well, you don't know me. But, I just had to! See how pretty she is! Who wouldn't go chasing after her? She was too perfect for me not to!" She smiled. "But you know Drew, sooner or later our decisions have consequences. Mine was sooner rather than later."

Carrie looked over her shoulder, back at God. He didn't utter a word, but the comfort in His eyes spoke volumes. Drew was clueless as to what they both knew, but he had never felt serenity as strongly as he did in that very moment.

"Hold her", Carrie encouraged.

Drew held out his hand, and the butterfly flapped her wings and softly landed on his thumb. He brought her closer and allowed her wings to fan his face. He closed his eyes and smiled. The wind from the butterfly produced a sweet fragrance that filled Drew's nostrils. "What is this that I smell?"

"Oh, it's my favorite perfume. Sweet Patches, it's called. I was wearing it the day I found her." She lowered her head and smiled.

"Well, it smells good."

"It does, doesn't it? Come! Climb up with me, and don't worry about falling. Nothing breaks here. Not even hearts!"

This girl is weird yet interesting, Drew thought, as he followed her lead.

Butterflies floated away, giving the two a perfect spot to land their feet. As they climbed higher, Drew thought how incredible this entire experience had been. He wondered if the trip would have happened if he had never been introduced to God by Nana and Grandpa. He questioned why his own parents had never taken him to church or referenced God, except for when it was time for dinner. Even then, Drew was the one responsible for saying grace. Never them. Drew paused as he looked into the far distance to where God still stood.

"God, why doesn't everyone accept and believe in You?" Drew spoke in a low tone, somehow knowing that God would hear him no matter the distance.

"Your question has no simple answer." God's voice was loud and audible. "There are many children who are not taught by their parents to believe in Me or to worship Me. Those children become adults and are spiritually bankrupt. They are lost unless someone else guides them to Me. Then, there are those who are taught about me as children, but when something sad or devastating happens in their life, they angrily decide that I am no longer worthy of being recognized. They decide that I do not exist. They march to the beat of their own drum, looking and searching for a pure peace that they will never find except through Me.

"Can you force them to love you and worship You?" Drew now longed for his parents to know this God.

"Of course I could. But when I created mankind, I gave them power to choose. People have the choice to believe and do what they want. It is my desire that they not fight their natural inclination to build a relationship with Me, but many do."

"Come," said Carrie. "We're almost to the top." She reached the highest branch, then Drew shortly after. She looked at him with excitement, then crawled onto the short branch. Drew carefully took a seat beside her and they both looked out at the breathtaking view. Carrie must've climbed this tree a million times, Drew thought, because she did it without effort and as if she'd never known fear. The sparkle in her big brown eyes was as if she had invited a guest into her home, and was proud to show him the view from the top floor. Their legs dangled from the branch while she pointed out Saturn and Mars in the far distance. There was a hint of sadness when she pointed out Earth, but it didn't last long. She continued pointing out the stars that fascinated her, then her attention returned to her favorite things—her butterflies. She had a special relationship with them, it seemed. As they sat and talked, the butterflies flew about as if captivated by what Carrie had to share. They made her smile. Watching her made Drew smile. What is it with this girl? He wondered.

"Why do I feel like I know you already Carrie?" It was something about her that he couldn't quite put his finger on. Her long and wavy black hair was pulled into a loose pony tail. Her lips were full and perfectly symmetrical, and her big brown eyes were surrounded by the longest lashes. He couldn't tear his eyes away from her.

"We've never met before, Drew." She giggled.

"Well, I'm not sure about that! And what's so funny?"

"I'm just so happy that Abba brought you here to meet me, that's all." Her voice was raspy, not like anyone's voice he'd ever heard. Maybe they hadn't met before.

"Well since I don't *know* you, Carrie, tell me a little about yourself. I know you like butterflies."

"Correction, I absolutely LOVE butterflies! Major difference! There are roughly 25,000 species of them on earth. They can only see 3 colors: red, green, and yellow. Most of them only live 2 to 3 weeks before transitioning here. The most interesting butterflies to me are the Peacock Pansy, Goliath Birdwing, Monarchs, and of course, my all-time favorite, the Blue Morpho from the Morphini Tribe." She laughed and instinctively batted her lashes at him as a Blue Morpho landed on her shoulder. "They call me the butterfly whisperer!" she teased. "You don't get that title by just *liking* butterflies!"

Drew was rendered speechless after hearing her rattle off butterfly facts so effortlessly. "Okay... I guess that's all I know about you. Tell me more." He was eager to hear how she got to live in a special place like this.

"Oh, here's something about me. Besides butterflies, I love horses too!"

"Really?"

"Oh, I do! Have you ever ridden one, Drew?"

"No, but we live close to a horse ranch. It's kinda cool to pass by and see them galloping."

"Oh that's great! You know, when Abba created animals, he gave a few of them the most incredible gift of helping people when they hurt inside." She motioned her hand in a circular motion around her heart. "Horses have that gift. These magnificent creatures don't speak our language, but they connect with us through our emotions. They feel what we feel. So you can't pretend around them. They force you to acknowledge what you're feeling, so that you can deal with it. Isn't that so cool? They make you T3."

"They make you what?"

"Horses! They make you T3... TELL THE TRUTH!" She laughed. "I came up with that one on my own." She hesitated, then continued. "I think Abba took a piece of Himself and put it in each of them. That's why they are so exquisitely sensitive and brilliant. I love horses!" God listened to the conversation with delight. Suddenly, Carrie's eyes flew open wide, as if she had a bright idea. "Oh Abba, may I take Drew on a ride?"

"Sure, Carrie. I knew you would want to, but it mustn't take long."

"Oh, thank you Abba!" She turned to Drew. "You aren't afraid are you?"

"So... there are horses here?"

"Of course there are. Small ones, big ones, black ones, brown ones!" She motioned for Drew to follow her down from the tree. There waiting at the base were two brown saddle horses. Drew did a double-take. "No way! How did these get here?"

"Abba did it! He's fast, huh!" She giggled more. It made Drew laugh too. "C'mon, let's ride!"

"Uh Carrie, there's a problem. I don't know the first thing about riding horses."

"No worries. I'll give you a quick lesson."

CHAPTER EIGHT

Within no time, instruction was complete, and both were on their individual horses riding away.

"This trip has been unbelievable. My meeting with God and now I am literally riding a horse, here in..."

Carrie waited for him to complete his sentence, but he hesitated. "Go on! Don't be afraid to say it! You are literally riding a horse where?"

Drew looked at her, and finally said, "Heaven?"

Carrie smiled. "That's right Drew! You are in Heaven! Not many people get a guest pass to visit here."

"I don't understand why God brought me here, but I'm glad He did."

"You won't always understand why Abba does what He does. But in time, it'll all become crystal clear. You just have to trust Him."

Drew was impressed with how wise this Carrie was.

"I wanna show you something, but we mustn't be long. Follow me." Her horse began to gallop and Drew's horse followed. It was his first ride on a horse, and there was no fear; only an intense feeling of euphoria.

As Carrie's horse galloped, her long thick pony-tail swung from side to side. She soon slowed her horse's pace, and motioned for Drew to bring his horse beside hers. She looked at Drew, then proudly pointed into the direction of what appeared to be a very large city. The streets were of a shiny substance and the houses were huge. The people here appeared happy as they danced and sang. It looked like one big celebration taking place.

"Carrie, what's the occasion? What are they celebrating?"

"Life Drew." She answered with pride. "Life after death."

At the end of the main street, Drew noticed a spectacular gate that kept opening and closing. He noticed a crowd standing on the inside in anticipation of someone. Each time it opened, many would walk through, some hugging someone who was already inside. Carrie could tell by Drew's face that he had several more questions.

"The ones you see walking through the gate are new to Heaven. When I first came here, I walked through those same gates." Drew looked at Carrie as if for the first time.

"So Carrie, you are... dead?"

She gazed at him as she sat upright on her horse. "Look at it this way. I used to live on Earth, but now I live here. Doesn't that sound better?"

Drew turned away from her with a heavy heart. Suddenly, his horse started moving about in a frantic manner.

"Hey, what's happening here?"

"She's reacting to your emotions, Drew. Look at me! I'm okay. I am very happy here!" Drew's horse continued swaying, her tail swishing from left to right.

"What happened to you? Why are you here?" A myriad of reasons buzzed about in his head. Carrie searched for the right words to comfort and calm him, but her thoughts kept getting interrupted by his ever increasing emotionally charged words. "Did... someone... hurt... you? Were you killed by someone, like a bully?" Huh? Before she could respond, another dreadful thought came to his mind.

"Carrie, did Luke kill you? Huh? Is that why God brought me here?" Drew's horse was now rearing up, as if in distress. He didn't care. He just held on tighter to the reigns, while the tears he'd imprisoned for months now celebrated their release.

"No, Drew! Listen to me! No one hurt me, okay!" Tears began welling up in her own eyes.

"Well? Just tell me, please! What happened to you?" The ugly display of tears and air-sucking continued. He needed answers.

"It was an accident! That's why I'm here, okay... an accident! But being here is not punishment. It is the ultimate gift God gives to His children who honors Him on earth. So... so although an accident happened on Earth, this is the new life God granted me, and I'm grateful for it!" She looked around at the city, back towards the meadow where God waited, then back to Drew. "I'm good here!"

Drew's heaving lessened as he glanced all around. The gate kept swinging open. The people in the city continued celebrating. He turned back to Carrie, who was having a difficult time controlling her tears.

"Carrie, am I... am I dead? Is that the reason He brought me here?"

Carrie laughed in spite of her tears. "Drew! Don't be ridiculous! Did you walk through those gates over there? Huh?"

Feeling silly, he said, "Well, no... "

"No! You are a guest here, okay!" Her smile faded. The tears continued.

"Carrie, I'm really sorry. I didn't mean to make you cry."

"It's okay. It's okay. Abba warned me that this might happen."

"He told you that I would make you cry?"

"No! He told me that the longer you were here, the stronger some emotions that died with me would become." She paused. "I'm feeling sadness because you're sad… and hanging with you all this time makes me miss my family. Truth is, I started missing them the moment I saw you." Drew would've given anything to know more about her life on earth and about her family. However, he decided to give it a rest; it wasn't worth making her sadder.

"Carrie, hanging here with you has really made me happy. I'm really sorry I had to go messing things up with all the questions… just trying to figure it all out. That's all."

"Just trust Abba, okay. He knows what He's doing. Come. We need to head back now."

Drew's horse was calm again as they made their way back. Carrie and Drew were quiet. They knew they would have to say goodbye soon. The sadness lingered like the dark cloud Nana saw the day God gave her a sign. Carrie stole a glance at him then decided to steer her horse closer to his.

"Hey! I've got a joke for you."

"Oh yeah… let me hear it."

"Okay, listen closely! A man needed a horse for traveling, so he went in search of one. He eventually stumbled upon a "horse for sell" sign. The horse seller said, "He's my last one, and I'm selling him for a good price. But there's something you need to know about my horse if you decide to buy him. He only responds to two commands—hallelujah and thank you Jesus! To make him go you must say, 'thank you Jesus', but to make him stop, you have to say 'hallelujah'. So the

man said, "Simple enough", and bought the horse
right then. To make the horse continue trotting, he
repeated *"Thank you Jesus"* over and over again.
Soon the horse was galloping at a fast pace, but the
cowboy realized he'd made a wrong turn and was
fast approaching a steep cliff. But the obedient horse
could only follow two orders. The cowboy said, *'Stop
boy stop!'* But the horse kept trotting. The cowboy
panicked! 'Oh goodness what's the other command?
What's the other command?' He said, *'GLORY*...
horse kept going! *'AMEN'*... kept going! Then at the
absolute final second, when they were at the very edge
of the cliff, the cowboy shouted, *'HALLELUJAH'*!
And the horse stopped just in the nick of time. The
happy cowboy wiped the sweat from his forehead, and
said, *'Thank you Jesus!'*... and they went overboard!"
Carrie cradled her stomach in laughter; Drew joined
in. He loved the joke but loved her laughter more.
Soon, the sadness returned like pesky mosquitos on a
hot summer day in Texas.

Carrie held out her hand. Drew grabbed it, and they
rode in silence towards the Almighty, who awaited
their return. When they arrived, Carrie dismounted
first, then quickly went over to help Drew.

"So how did I do teacher?"

"Not bad cowboy! Not bad at all! You just might be
ready for your first rodeo!" She giggled, giving him a
hug. Drew held on tightly.

"I'm gonna miss you somethin' terrible!"

Carrie pulled slightly away with a curious look on her face. "Where'd you learn that old-fogey phrase?"

"Ha! It's what my grandma says to me when I'm leaving her house or when she's leaving mine."

"Well, I'm gonna miss you somethin' terrible too!" She forced a smile, but her emotions were getting the best of her. Heavy tears started flowing from her sad eyes. "Hey, I want you to do me a big favor." She wiped at her tears.

"Okay... what's that?"

She composed herself, then whispered her request into his ear. Drew's eyes widened. The request was baffling to him.

"Wait, what? I don't understand!"

She smiled the sweetest smile, but had no intention of offering an explanation. "I had fun hanging with you Andrew. Enjoy life on earth, okay! And hey... don't be afraid to discover things that others have not, Mr. Scientist! Live boldly, but follow the rules! See you later!" She walked over to God and fell into His majestic embrace, sobbing loudly into His chest. God's eyes were closed as He consoled her. When He released her from His embrace, she appeared the way she did when Drew first saw her—happy with no cares in the world. The tears had disappeared.

"Thank You Abba! I love You!"

"I love you more, My child."

She blew Drew a kiss then ran off into the field with her entourage of butterflies. He watched her until she disappeared in the tall grassy field. The smell of her perfume lingered in the air. The sweet scent of jasmine with a tiny hint of patchouli was all over his clothes. Sweet Patches, she called it. It was the first time Drew didn't mind smelling like perfume.

Drew turned away from the field, unable to concentrate on anything but the memory of this intriguing girl named Carrie, and the curious thing she had just whispered into his ear. He shook his head, then turned to God who had His hand extended. Drew grabbed it without hesitation. Being close to Him made Drew feel complete, but he wished that he could somehow become a three year old again so that he could throw a tantrum and scream, "I don't wanna go bye-bye! I wanna stay right here!" He knew that wouldn't be acceptable.

"Where to now, God?"

"Back to our meeting on the moon!"

In a blink of an eye, they were back to where the meeting had started.

CHAPTER NINE

T hen God said, "Drew, I believe I've satisfied all of your questions. Haven't I?"

"Yes Sir, I believe so." There was so much more Drew could talk to God about, like who Carrie was and why God had arranged their meeting. But Drew didn't want to take up more of His time. Besides, he figured God had other prayers to answer and other miracles to perform.

"Before you go... " God started.

"God, I don't wanna go! I mean... I'm not ready! Not yet, at least. Can I stay just a little while longer? It feels good to be in Your presence. I feel safe here." He looked up at God with pleading eyes.

"My son, you can't stay here. Besides, there are things that you must tend to when you get home." Drew knew what God was referring to. Just thinking of Luke made him sad and thinking of his father evoked the same emotion.

"Once you have addressed your problems, I have a special task that I desire for you to carry out. There are things I want you to tell my people."

Drew looked up at God in confusion. "See, I've failed already, because I don't even know who *Your people* are!"

"I created everyone, Drew! But the message will be to those who know me, and those who desire a relationship with me."

"So, You want me, an eleven year old kid, to tell Your people something?"

"That is correct! Thousands that you encounter in your lifetime will be blessed when you share My message."

"I'm not sure how I would make that happen. What if I let you down?"

"I don't expect perfection Drew; I only want your best. As long as you don't allow fear to paralyze you, you'll be just fine. Fear will alter your destiny and potentially impact the destiny of others. So trust in Me, and I will give you the confidence and strength you need to push through fear."

"I don't understand it all, but whatever You want me to do, I'll do it!"

God was pleased. They walked about the moon while God shared with Drew what He wanted him to tell His people. Drew took it all in, asking for clarification when necessary.

"Enough for now. I'll share more with you in time."

"Yes, sir." Drew glanced around, taking in the moon and all its splendor. It was definitely an amazing place. No trip would ever compare to this one, he thought. He looked down at his feet, and thought how lucky he was to be where he stood.

"Think fast!" At that moment, God playfully threw a small moon rock to Drew. He instinctively caught it! "Ball's in your court now!" God said.

Drew forced a smiled as he studied the rock. He knew that his trip had come to an end.

"We won't ever meet like this again, huh?"

"No. Not like this Drew, but when you assemble with others to worship Me, you will feel My presence. When you hear and see the ocean waves, that'll be Me. When you see the trees blowing in the wind, or feel the warmth of the sunshine, that'll be Me. When you feel the raindrops on your head or see the snowflakes outside your window... Me. When you see the stars above twinkle and the soft glow from this very moon that you love so much...

"It'll be You!"

"It'll be Me! Always remember that when you need guidance, read the manual I left for My people. Nana and Grandpa gave you one for your last birthday." Drew couldn't remember ever opening his bible to read it, but things would change when he got home, he thought. He placed the rock in his pocket and in a ceremonial fashion, he fell to his knees and bowed in front of the Almighty.

"My father who art in Heaven.

Hallowed be Thy name.

Thy Kingdom come. Thy will be done, on earth, as it is in Heaven.

Give us this day our daily bread, and forgive us our trespasses.

As we forgive those who trespass against us.

Lead me not into temptation, but deliver me from the evil one.

For Thine is the kingdom, and the power, and the glory, forever and ever...

Thank you Father for loving me, your child, and allowing this trip to take place. Thank you for what You've shown me today, and although I don't understand it all, I trust You. I know You will reveal more to me when the time is right. I look forward to learning more about You and your Son when I return home. And for as long as I live, I promise to stand boldly and tell the world that I know You. In Jesus' name I pray, Amen."

God reached down, and laid His mighty hand on Drew's head. Drew welcomed the surge of energy coursing through his veins. "I bless You My child. Rest well and remember, I will be with you."

Drew felt tired. So tired. He started drifting into a deep slumber, his body slowly descending from the moon. It was the sensation of being on a descending roller coaster, except slower. His body twisted and turned. There were familiar echoes in his ear. *I'll be with you. Live boldly! You're the scum of the earth! Go to your room! Hallelujah! Thank you Jesus! I'll see you later*! Horses galloped past him; butterflies and kick balls floated about his head. Moment after moment passed until finally, a safe landing in the small town of Solome where it all started.

Chapter Ten

"**G**ood morning sweetheart." Andrew Sr. planted a kiss on his wife's cheek as she stirred the grits on the stove.

"And good morning to you." She smiled. "Breakfast will be done soon. The bacon just needs one more minute." The biscuits and eggs were already done.

"Smells good."

"Thanks!"

"It's 10:30. Has Drew been down yet?"

"Nope, not a peep."

"Man! He must've had a pretty rough week at school then. Is that even normal? Coming home from school and sleeping until the next day?"

"He's a growing boy just taking advantage of his weekend." She remembered how weary he looked when he got home, but she didn't want to worry her husband about that. Besides, she had something else to share with him that might cause more concern.

"Well, he won't be happy when he sees that I brought home Congo's Pizza last night. What was I thinking anyways, rewarding him after all that smack he talked the other night?"

Karen grinned as she removed the bacon from the pan onto a small platter. "I know, right! But there's still a few slices in the fridge, if he wants some for later."

"That's good, I guess."

"Hey babe, on another note. I went to check on him this morning. He was still asleep, but I noticed that his window was raised."

"Huh? That's impossible. It's too difficult to raise those storm windows without help. Besides, the alarm would've sounded."

"Honey, I know, but I'm telling you what I saw. His window was fully raised, and the alarm did not go off." Just then, Drew walked in.

"Good morning Mom and Dad."

Karen looked Drew over, and thought how refreshed he looked. He stood upright as if he had the confidence of a decorated soldier. Even the knot on his head was gone. Must've been the clean night air that entered his room, she thought.

"Good morning son." She hugged him.

Andrew Sr. was too busy scratching his head to speak. He pushed away from the table, then bolted upstairs.

"Uh, what's wrong with him?"

She leaned against the countertop, her arms folded across her chest. "Drew, when I came to your room earlier this morning, I noticed that your window was raised. How were you able to open such a heavy window on your own, and without the alarm going off? I mean, did you somehow manipulate the security box so that the alarm wouldn't sound? Maybe we didn't program it for your room."

Drew decided that he'd let her carry on until she'd satisfied her own inquiry.

"But that can't be, because I'm pretty sure we double-checked. But maybe we didn't. Did you have difficulty opening the window? I mean, you were the one who opened it, right? Drew?"

Hmmm... How do I answer that question? Drew thought. As he calmly pondered his response, Andrew Sr. returned to his seat in the kitchen, with a confused expression. Drew decided this would be a good time for him to sit as well. He had no plans to divulge the details of his meeting so early, but it looked like they were leaving him no choice. They needed answers about the window this morning.

"Okay, Mom and Dad. There is an explanation about the window, and I will try to explain as best I can. But I haven't eaten since last night and I'm starved! So can we just start eating breakfast first? I promise I'll explain in a moment."

More puzzled looks.

"Wait... so you did come down last night to eat some of the pizza Dad bought?"

"Dad bought pizza?"

Karen just stared at her son, not sure how to continue. She chose not to answer Drew. She was afraid to because she knew she'd have to follow-up with another question, such as, "If you didn't eat the pizza, then what did you eat? And how did you get there?" She was afraid of what he would he say and what his father's response would be. So those questions would not come from her lips. She was well aware of the distance between the two of them, but dismissed it as a phase that would soon end. She'd questioned Andrew, Sr. on several occasions, but he always blamed it on stress from work. She knew it was more, because sometimes in the middle of the night, when he thought she was asleep, she could hear him crying in another room. She had a hunch about what it might be, but he would never entertain her. So she thought it would be best to leave well enough alone. But now, she was feeling uneasy.

Drew had devoured a good portion of his breakfast when he decided that he'd better start talking before his mother passed out from holding her breath or before his father pulled him clear across the table by his shirt demanding an answer. He sat his fork down, and slowly pushed his plate away. He cleared his throat, then looked at his father who appeared angry and then to his mom who looked worried.

"What I have to tell you guys may not be easy to hear or believe, but all of it is true." He paused not knowing how to proceed. He took a deep breath and decided to just say what came to mind first. "Okay, so there's this kid who's been bullying me since the beginning of school."

Karen gasped, as she raised a hand to cover her mouth.

If she's gasping now, Drew thought, she'll be on the floor passed out by the time I tell her the rest.

"Mom I'm okay! At least now I am. At first I didn't know what to do, because this boy always said he'd hurt me more if I told an adult. So I didn't. I tried to handle it on my own, but it kept getting worse. I was pretty sure he'd kill me, and that it would happen during school."

Andrew Sr.'s expression went from anger to one of concern. He placed his hand under his chin, eager to hear more.

"What did he do to you, Drew?" It pained Karen to know that something terrible was going on with him, and she ignored the signs.

"Lots of things, Mom. When it started getting bad, I wanted to tell you so many times Dad, but lately it's been hard to talk to you. Every time I try… well, you always say it's not a good time or that you've had a long day at work or something."

"Why didn't you just come to me Drew?" Tears clouded her eyes.

"Mom, the baby keeps you busy. I didn't want to burden you with stuff like this. Besides, it was something I wanted Dad to help me with. But when I couldn't get him to talk to me," he lowered his head, "I prayed and asked God to meet me... and He did." He squinted to see their expressions.

"Oh wow, come here baby. Are you okay?" Karen got up and placed her hand on his forehead. Something had to be wrong with him to make such a ridiculous statement, she thought.

Drew leaned his head over and away from her hand. "Mom I'm not sick, and I'm not crazy! I'm actually better than I've ever been." He calmly replied.

"Son, what are you talking about? A meeting?" Andrew Sr. wanted more details, as he stared at this boy that looked just like him when he was about the same age.

"I promise you this will sound crazy... but every bit of it is true. I met God on the moon last night!"

"Oh dear God!" Karen was now feeling her own head. "Drew baby, you've gotta be talking about a dream, right?" Drew ignored her question and continued. He was determined not to doubt his experience.

"Like I said, the meeting was last night. He– God– was the One who opened the window for me to get to the moon.

His father set back in his chair, folded his arms, and smirked. "Son you have lost your ever loving mind!"

"Honey, calm down before you wake the baby. Just let him talk, for crying out loud!" She rolled her eyes, feeling irritated with him.

"What do you mean, calm down? You think this is crazy talk too, otherwise you wouldn't be feeling on his head! Son, I admit that I haven't been the best father lately. I'll admit that, and I know I need to do better. Alright? But to make up this... this story all willy-nilly to get my attention is totally unnecessary and downright ridiculous! Did one of your friends tell you to come up with this tall tale? Or did you read it somewhere in one of your geeky magazines? Huh?"

"Andrew, stop it!"

"Karen, we asked the boy a simple question about the window, and he tells us that he met God on the moon because I wouldn't talk to him! Does anyone else think that's crazy besides me?"

Drew sat there looking at the table, trying to keep calm by thinking of something else. He thought about his brief time in Heaven with Carrie and how much he missed her. When there was silence, he continued. He decided to leave out the part about eating pizza on the moon, figuring that part would send his father through the roof. Then, he thought they'd be quick to say that he slept walk last night and ate some of the pizza from his own kitchen. For a moment Drew pondered the possibility, but quickly dismissed it.

He cleared his throat again. "God knows how much I love the moon, so He was kind enough to meet me there. We talked about lots of things during our meeting, mainly Luke." He looked up at them. "Luke is the kid who's been bullying me."

"So what did... uh... God have to say about Luke the bully? Hmmm?" Although he lowered his voice, there was a hint of sarcasm in Andrew Sr.'s question.

"Well, He actually showed me a video of what goes on in Luke's house. After seeing it, it made me kind of understand why Luke is a bully. I'm not sure why he chose me to hurt, but I understand why he is a bully. I was really starting to hate this kid, but I don't anymore. I feel sad for him now. He really needs help."

"What did the dream... I mean... what did God show you in this video?" Karen asked.

"It showed Luke being hurt really bad by his stepdad. His mother can't help him because she is in bed dying. The things that Luke calls me at school are the same things I heard his stepdad call him on the video. It was so weird. It's like Luke's becoming Phil. That's his stepdad's name."

"Has anyone ever told you anything about Luke's life before... before your meeting?"

"Nothing at all, Mom."

"So what else happened on the moon, after you all left my window open?" The mockery in his father's tone continued. Drew looked up at him, the anger in his eyes still evident.

"God told me a lot of things that He wants me to share with His people."

His parents looked at each other.

"How do you plan to do that? Did He give you a plan?"

"No, He didn't. He just said that He would be with me the entire time."

"Drew, have you talked to Nana anytime lately?"

"No sir. Not since her birthday in August. Why?"

"Don't worry about it. Just continue. What else happened in your *meeting*? Did you talk about me?"

Drew looked down, but nodded in affirmation.

Andrew Sr. slapped his leg. "Hot doggit! This is gettin' good! So what did He say about me? Huh? This will be interesting to hear!"

"Well, God said lots of things, but mainly that you love me and that you and I are going to be okay."

Andrew Sr. suddenly felt a lump in his throat. He looked down while he gained his composure. In his rule book, crying was only allowed in private.

"God said it, and I believe it!"

"Son, I believe that too. But what I am having a problem believing is this far-fetched story about meeting God on the moon. If God is really real, I don't think He'd have the time to be meeting people, and certainly not on the moon. I mean, maybe I'd halfway believe your story if you told us that you died and went to Heaven and met Him there or something. But the moon son?"

"Well… "

"Well what?" Andrew Sr. yelled.

"Believe it or not, I saw Heaven too."

"Wow. This is getting gooder and gooder!" His father sat back in his chair and threw his hands up, as if in defeat.

There was a distant whimpering coming from the nursery.

"Let me get the baby. Drew, don't say another word until I get back." At this point, his mom was totally enthralled by Drew's story. Whether it was true or not, she thought he was a great story-teller, and was eager to hear more.

Drew and Andrew Sr. sat at the table in silence. Hurry back Mom, he thought. The tension in the room was so thick, it could be sliced and served to the neighbors. Drew fiddled with his fingers, and decided not to look across the table at his father who still had his arms folded, tapping his right foot. Drew was undecided about what additional parts to share with them. He continued fiddling. He could feel his father's stare. *Why is he so angry?*

Karen returned with Sophia. Her loose curls were in disarray, her smile was toothless, but she was still the cutest baby in the world to her big brother. For a brief moment, Drew ignored the stress he felt from the inquisition to admire Sophia's big brown eyes and her long eye lashes. Almost instantly, he felt butterflies in his stomach, as there was a striking resemblance between Sophia and Carrie.

"Oh wow, baby girl! This is crazy! You look a lot like someone I met in Heaven! Yes, you do!" Drew had slid out of his seat and was on his knees, eye level with the baby as she sat on Karen's lap. Sophia grabbed Drew's face and gave him an open mouth kiss. "I love you baby girl, but that's a lotta spit!" He wiped his mouth with the back of his hand, kissed her forehead, then returned slowly to the hot seat.

"So you met someone... in Heaven?"

"I did! I still haven't figured out why, but God took me there to meet her." He smiled and shook his head. "That girl... I have never met anyone like her before, and I'll never forget her as long as I live. God let me hang with her for a little while. She was so funny and full of energy. For some reason I felt like I knew her, but turns out I'd never met her before." He looked at the baby again. "But this is crazy how Sophia kind of looks like her. Maybe that's why I felt I knew her!"

Both Andrew Sr. and Karen looked at each other nervously. They both had a new found urgency to hear more of Drew's story.

"Does this girl live there or was she just visiting like you?" Karen tried remaining calm, as she could feel her heart in her throat.

"No, she lives there now." He put his head down. "I'm not exactly sure what happened to her, but I know Heaven is now her home. I had a lot of fun with her.

God allowed her to show me all around. We climbed a tree and she showed me all these butterflies that she loves so much. She even taught me how to ride a horse!" Karen's heart was beating a mile a minute. Andrew Sr.'s felt like his wanted to stop.

"Son, did this girl... that you met in Heaven tell you her name?" Karen rocked back and forth in her chair pretending to soothe Sophia, but it was all for her own benefit. The men in her life seemed to be unraveling right before her eyes and the answer to this question was about to make it worse.

"Her name was Carrie, the butterfly whisperer!"

When Andrew Sr. heard Drew's answer, the room started spinning. "Son, where did this story come from? Huh? Did someone tell you to tell us these things? If you tell me where it came from, I swear you won't be in any trouble!" Drew was scared.

"No one told me to say these things. It's really what happened to me last night. Why is this so upsetting to you? Do you know my friend, Carrie?"

"Oh God! Son, I need you to go to your room!" He couldn't hide it any longer. Andrew Sr. grabbed his head and started weeping. The invisible wall that he had built was finally crumbling and he felt exposed. Drew started to cry too, because it was now apparent to him that the cries he heard at night were those of his father. His heart sank.

"Dad what's wrong? What did I say?" He never imagined that the details of his meeting would cause this level of turmoil.

"Everybody please, just calm down!" Karen walked back and forth, holding the baby close to her.

"Dad, why am I being sent to my room for telling the truth?" Drew suddenly remembered the strange message that Carrie had whispered in his ear.

"Don't question me! I said go to your room, and I mean now!"

Drew stood, trying to appear tall, brave, and unconfused. After all, no one should be a wimp after meeting God face to face. "Okay, I'm going! But just tell me one thing. Who is she Dad? Huh? Who is Carrie to you? You must know her, and she must know you too, be... because she gave me a message to deliver to you!"

Karen gasped, "Oh dear God!" She couldn't take it any longer. She took a seat, before Drew's next words delivered a blow to both her knees.

Andrew Sr. was dizzy. He held on tight to the back of the chair, before finally making his way to the front of it to sit. He rested his elbows on his knees as he cradled his head in his hands. This can't be true, he thought. It can't be. Someone was playing a dirty trick on him, and was using his own son as a pun in their evil scheme.

"She had a message for me? What did she say?"

"She said, 'Tell your dad hello for me, and that I'm okay. Tell him that I love him very much and that what happened that day was not his fault.' Who is she to you, Dad?"

Andrew Sr. looked up to answer Drew, but he could no longer see. His sight had failed him. "My little sister... Carrie was my little sister!" He collapsed onto the floor.

CHAPTER ELEVEN

The seats in the emergency room were hard and uncomfortable, much like the conversation at the Carmichael's that morning. The room was large and rectangular in shape. Single seats lined the walls while three rows of back-to-back seats took center stage. With ample seating, only four waited to be seen. A young lady and a small baby boy sat close to the far wall. The baby seemed healthy, except for the cough that was reminiscent of a motor cycle being started. That couldn't be good, Drew thought. Sitting at the opposite end of that same row was an elderly man and his adult daughter. He rocked back and forth as he held firmly to the white blanket draped around him. Drew overheard the daughter telling the front desk lady that his fever would not come down, and that his shivering would not cease. Then there was the teenage girl who held a cold pack to her forehead. Judging by the soccer uniform she wore, Drew concluded that her head must've collided with another player's, resulting in a concussion. Her mother sat on one side of her; her dad the other. Finally, there was a lady with her left hand wrapped in a blood-stained towel. Cooking accident. Her friend sitting beside her draped his arm around her shoulder for consolation. Drew sat alone watching and waiting.

Ms. Theresa from next door had agreed to take care of Sophia while Karen and Drew followed the ambulance to City Bend Hospital. When they arrived, Karen decided that Drew should wait in the wait-room; he didn't argue. He was emotionally drained, and needed a mental break anyway, but the events leading up to the emergency room kept replaying in his head. He didn't imagine that life after the meeting would be so immediately chaotic and overwhelming. Did the meeting really happen, he wondered, or was it figments of a dream brought on by a crazy school day? Just maybe the pizza he ate last night did indeed come from his own kitchen, and not courtesy of God on the moon. He shook his head and immediately dismissed the thoughts again. It had to be real; otherwise, he wouldn't be sitting in an emergency room because his father lost consciousness due to compelling details he shared from the meeting.

Sister? "Carrie is my father's sister?" he mumbled to himself. What a revelation! There was so much more Drew wanted to know about Carrie. About that day she died. However, he'd have to wait until the unconscious one felt up to talking. There was to be no pushing for information, as instructed by his mom. "He needs to process everything you've shared with us", Karen had advised on the way to the emergency room. She too had been spooked, and needed time to swallow Drew's information. The remainder of the trip had been made in silence.

Drew sat back in his cold chair and smiled as he thought about how magnificent God was for allowing him to visit a place he never imagined he'd get to see so soon. He felt grateful for gaining an understanding about Luke, the one whose life's mission it was to torture him at school. Then God allowed him to meet the mysterious Carrie. As he stared at the floor searching for answers, his thoughts were interrupted by a familiar pair of sneakers worn by someone checking in at the front desk. He held his breath as he looked up to confirm his fears. It was Luke and standing next to him was Phil.

Drew scooted down into his seat and grabbed a magazine from the seat next to him and held it high to shield his face. Why was he here, he thought. His heart felt like it was beating outside his chest. "Calm down Drew, calm down. God said he wouldn't hurt you anymore." Drew held the magazine down low enough to see the enemy and the enemy's enemy. Luke was holding his right arm with his left. Phil talked to the receptionist, while Luke rocked from side to side, as if the repetitive motion would somehow calm the pain he was experiencing.

When they were done at the desk, Phil and Luke turned to look for seats. Drew's heart seemed to pound harder as he raised the magazine higher. Panic consumed him. Please don't sit by me! Please don't sit by me! Go somewhere else, he thought. He realized that being in Luke's presence made him feel worthless and like dirt. Weekends are supposed to be a break from bullies, he thought. *You're not supposed to be here! Go home!* After a moment, Drew lowered the magazine to see where Luke and his stepdad planted themselves. They sat in seats far behind Drew; against the wall and near the door. Luke's head was down. This was the perfect time to move to another seat; farther away from him. He chose a chair against another wall, but closer to the front desk. That way, he could watch Luke's every move.

Based on Luke's pained expression, he posed no threat to Luke today. He and Phil sat with no exchange of words. Luke's head remained down, as he held his right arm close to his body. Spying on Luke in the waiting room reminded Drew of the video. Drew suddenly dismissed concern for himself and began to feel pity for Luke. Phil did something to him; Drew just knew it. Phil showed no signs of affection or concern for his stepson's arm. He only looked forward, appearing bothered by being there. After a while, he uttered something to Luke, then walked through the ER entrance. Luke's head remained down.

Through the window, Drew noticed Phil fishing for something in the pocket of his jacket. What emerged was a pack of cigarettes and a lighter. He lit the cigarette fast, and started taking long drags. Meanwhile Luke looked as if he had no hope; like if the floor opened and engulfed him, it wouldn't matter at all to him. Drew's heart sank. He felt like he needed to go over and be a friend to him. He tried convincing himself that he was out of his mind. *Victims shouldn't talk to their bullies! Victims can't be friends with people who hurt them! Victims should ignore the bad guys–let them take care of themselves!* Then out of nowhere he heard a small voice say,

"You are no longer a victim." And as if something had taken over Drew's mind and body, he stood up without further contemplation, walked boldly over, and sat beside the one who just one day before, had delivered excruciating blows to his body. This courage he felt was certainly unlike himself, but it felt right to be there, sitting next to his bully.

"Uhm... hi Luke."

Luke looked at him, frowned, and quickly turned away. "What are you doing here? And why on earth are you sitting next to me?"

Drew cleared his throat, and prayed that the courage that lead him there wouldn't go running out the ER entrance past Phil. "My dad didn't feel well this morning. Had to bring him here. Why are you here? What happened to your arm?"

"It's none of your freaking business!" He hissed as he kept his head down.

Drew paused for a moment, searching for the right things to say. Even at the age of eleven, he knew that this moment was critical, a moment he needed to make a small impact with Luke.

"Luke... "

"Get away from me before my stepdad comes back! You think I'm mean, he's far worse."

"I know all about your stepdad, Phil."

Luke was caught off guard. He didn't move or blink.

"I know that he hurts you with his hands, and that your mom can't defend you because she is so sick. I'm pretty sure he's the reason you're in the emergency room right now. Am I right?"

Luke was dumbfounded. His victim was mouthing off to him like he wasn't afraid of him anymore, like he had some newfound confidence. He responded between clenched teeth. "Listen, you don't know nothing about me or my life! So if you are as smart as they say you are, you'd get away from me fast before I spit on you!" Drew didn't move.

"Okay, I'll go back to my seat, but before I do, I want you to know that I forgive you for every horrible thing you've ever done to me. I'm not holding it against you anymore. I've wiped the slate clean." Luke hadn't spit on him yet, so he continued. "I also want you to know that God loves you, and He sent me to tell you that you're gonna be okay. That's a promise!"

Luke's mouth was slightly ajar in disbelief.

Drew decided this would be a good time to get up and walk away, but heard something he never thought he'd hear coming from Luke's mouth.

"Wait a minute. Come back... please!"

Drew glanced out the window as he walked back. Phil was fumbling for a second cigarette, so he sat down.

Luke quickly glanced at the entrance, then back to Drew. "Hey, who told you that stuff?"

"God did... and He also helped me understand why you've been mean to me. You were hurting me because it's what Phil does to you." Luke listened as he cradled his arm that pained him.

"I prayed for you last night, and God promised me that you were going to be okay. But don't block and delay the good things that are supposed to happen to you by lying. Just T3... tell the truth when it's time, so that things can change soon. You're gonna be okay buddy." *Buddy*? Drew couldn't believe that word had just escaped his mouth.

"God isn't real, you freak!" Luke's hope was depleting fast.

"Oh He's real alright! If He wasn't, I wouldn't be sitting beside you right now! Trust me!"

"Okay, I've heard enough of your nonsense! Go back to your seat now."

"Okay, I will. I hope your arm gets to feeling better. I'm happy about the changes that will be happening in your life soon." Drew walked away, hoping that what he said helped Luke. Shortly after taking his seat, Phil returned and took his seat beside Luke. Luke peeked up at Drew, and Drew formed the letter "t" with his pointer fingers and then held up three fingers. Luke stared at him for a brief moment, then turned away. Sharp pains were shooting through his broken arm.

"Luke Herman." The nurse holding a file scanned the room, then settled her eyes on Luke and Phil as they made their way towards her. "Come this way." Drew watched them as they disappeared through the double doors. He looked up, and thanked God for giving him the courage to talk to his bully, and prayed that God would give Luke the same courage to tell what's been going on at home.

CHAPTER TWELVE

D r. Pratt strolled into room 8, holding a manila folder with Andrew Carmichael, Sr. printed on the tab. After glancing over the contents one last time, he looked up and said, "Mr. Carmichael all of your test results have returned normal, confirming what I told you my suspicions were. Panic attack. So the good news is you get to go home."

"Oh thank Goodness!" said Karen, rubbing her husband's arm.

"Though I must say, whatever caused you to have this severe panic attack and subsequent syncope should not be ignored."

Andrew Sr. looked down, not wanting the doctor to see the guilt in his eyes.

"I advise you to take it easy when you get home. But stress needs an outlet. If exercising isn't part of your daily routine, you might want to incorporate it. And if there is some major stressor in your life that has become too much to handle alone, do yourself a favor and go talk to someone. The fact that you are here, in this emergency room, is a pretty clear indication that something needs to be dealt with."

"So it wasn't a heart attack?"

"No sir, but the symptoms of a heart attack and a panic attack are quite similar. Chest pains, shortness of breath, dizziness. However, your results point to a panic attack." Dr. Pratt looked down at the file in his hands. "You're 35 years old. Take care of your physical and emotional health so that you can be around for 35 plus years. You have any questions for me?"

"No sir. Thank you for everything."

"You bet."

The nurse came in shortly after, and gave him his discharge documents and a two day supply of anti-anxiety medication, just in case he had another attack before he consulted with his primary doctor.

As Andrew Sr. and Karen headed down the hall toward the exit doors, Luke and a nurse were approaching them, his arm now in a temporary arm sling for support. He looked at the Carmichaels and offered a polite smile as he passed by.

"After your x-ray, there will be a nice lady waiting to talk to you about what happened to your arm, okay?"

"Okay."

Karen, glanced back as they passed. "Poor guy. Sounds like somebody is in trouble for hurting him! Such a sweet face."

—◯—

Karen slowly pulled into the driveway, in the same fashion one would after being away from home for weeks. They looked the house over from top to bottom, searching for anything that seemed disturbed or out of place. They found nothing wrong. The front door was closed like it was when they left. All the front-facing windows, including Drew's, appeared to be closed and intact. Everything was the same. The only thing that had changed was them.

Following doctor's orders, Andrew Sr. went straight to their bedroom to lay down for a nap. Drew decided he needed a nap as well. Karen took a deep breath, then laid her purse and keys down on the sofa before heading next door to pick up Sophia. After returning, Karen sat on the floor with her and watched her play with her toys already scattered about. Two weeks before, Sophia had taken a few steps, but the day after she had refused to take any further steps. So she crawled from one toy to the next, then back to her mom. Karen welcomed the distraction. She did well focusing on Sophia but, periodically, her mind would drift back to the conversation over breakfast that resulted in her calling 911. She knew the conversation was just the tip of the iceberg, and thinking about it made her tired. She secretly asked this God to give her strength.

The phone rang. She rushed over to answer it, so that it wouldn't disturb Andrew Sr. and Drew.

"Hello."

"Mrs. Carmichael?"

"Yes."

"Hi. This is Ms. Crane, Andrew's teacher. How are you?"

"I'm good. Thank you. Is everything alright?" She had a feeling that it wasn't. She'd never received a phone call on the weekend from Drew's teacher.

"Well, there is a serious concern that has been brought to my attention, and I needed to contact you ASAP about it."

"Oh dear. What's the matter?"

"It's about one of Andrew's journal entries from last week."

"Okay?"

"He wrote a pretend newspaper article entitled, "11 Year Old Bully Kills Kid at School"."

"Oh father!"

"I won't read it to you, but based on the details of the article, I am convinced that he is being bullied by the kid he named in the story. We don't take information like this lightly. It is definitely a cry for help. I have already contacted my principal, and she has set into motion the district's no-bullying protocol to handle the situation expeditiously."

"Okay, thank you! I really appreciate it!"

"Just so you know, when I contacted Principal Baxter, she informed me that she had just received an email from a parent whose child has seen some of the bullying take place. This parent said that she attempted to contact you multiple times today on your cell phone, but only got your voicemail."

"We've had a hectic day today, and I haven't stopped to check my phone. It must be in silent mode."

She placed Sophia in her playpen, then grabbed her purse that was sitting on the sofa. She rummaged through it, then fished out her cell phone.

"I'm looking at my phone now. Yes, you're right. I've missed six calls from Cathy Jacobs."

"Yes. She is the one who contacted Mrs. Baxter. Mrs. Carmichael, were you aware of any of this? Did you see any signs? Had Andrew mentioned anything to you or your husband?"

Every muscle in Karen's body tightened more. "Drew told us this morning about this Luke. I don't know his last name. My plan was to visit the school Monday morning to discuss the situation with all of you. But before today, he'd never mentioned anything. It was only yesterday that I noticed bruising to his head and weird movement." Karen felt like a horrible mother, thinking that she should've noticed long before yesterday. "Will I be able to see this newspaper article he wrote when I meet with you all?"

"Absolutely", Ms. Crane replied. "In the meantime, give him extra love, and let him know that he won't have to worry about the bullying any longer. It is being taken care of."

"Thank you Ms. Crane. I look forward to meeting with you on Monday." She wished that she could give Ms. Crane a glimpse of everything that had transpired in her home that day, but she figured it wasn't necessary. Besides, how would she explain it when she had difficulty with the details herself?

Dinner time was quiet. Each of them had their own conversations playing in their heads as they ate. There was no need to share. It was safe that way. After a little while, Andrew Sr. broke the silence. "It's been a long day, huh family?" He faked a laugh. Karen smiled nervously at him. Drew was pleased to hear him laugh, even if it was forced.

"Son, thank you for sharing what you did this morning."

"No problem, Dad."

"Karen baby, I owe you an apology."

"For what, honey?"

"Well, since I've been neglecting my own issues, I've forced you to make up for my shortcomings in this family. For that, I'm sorry. Things won't change overnight, but I'm committed to the process starting today. "Son... " He hesitated while he chose his words carefully. "I don't know if my mind is ready to accept every single thing you shared this morning... but it's very clear to your mom and me that you experienced something extraordinary last night, whether it was a dream or reality. I want us to talk after dinner, if you're okay with that?"

"I'm more than okay with it." Drew smiled. He'd waited for weeks and months to hear his dad say something along those lines. It felt good to finally hear it.

Andrew Sr. cleared his throat as he choked back tears. "A conversation with you has been long overdue and I do apologize. Now about this bully at school... "

Drew was about to comment, but Karen interrupted. "It's already being taken care of. I talked to Ms. Crane while you slept and she has been made aware." She looked at her husband. "Honey, there's a meeting Monday morning. I'll give you more details later." She gave off strong vibes that she didn't want to tackle that subject. She feared any commentary from Drew right now would send them back to the same spooky abyss from this morning. Dealing with the message from Heaven was more than enough to process for quite a while.

Dinner was over. Drew decided to play with his baby sister in the living room. He had newfound admiration for her. He couldn't get over how much Sophia looked like the girl from Heaven—his dad's sister and their dead aunt. If she looked like Carrie now, she would certainly be the splitting image of her growing up, he thought. He hoped! He backed away from her and she'd crawl as fast as her little legs would allow to catch him! When she got to him, she'd grab hold of him and giggle. He picked her up and swung her around. He loved her so much. Karen interrupted their play time.

"Drew, your dad's ready to talk to you in our room." She kissed his forehead and grabbed the baby from him.

"Wish me luck!" He winked at her.

When Drew walked in, he found his father sitting on the sofa in the bedroom's sitting area.

Parked on the coffee table, in front of him, was an old cardboard box that had "DO NOT OPEN" boldly inscribed on all sides. Written on top was "CC". Sitting right beside the box was medication from the emergency room. Drew hoped that he had taken the latest dose of whatever had been prescribed. He wanted this talk to start and end well.

"Come. Have a seat, Drew." His tone was calm and welcoming. Drew was pleased. He took a seat right beside him. The two sat in silence for a while. Drew had spilled most of his guts to them this morning. It was his father's turn to talk now. Andrew Sr. wiped at his eyes twice, then he started to talk.

"I owe you an apology for being a jerk! Not just today, but for the last few months you've needed me and I've been an absentee father. I'm really, really sorry."

"Dad it's okay. I forgive you."

"What you shared today... whew! It wasn't easy to hear, especially for someone like me. Apparently, I needed that meeting to happen just as much as you did. I think the entire Carmichael family needed the meeting to happen!" He wiped away another tear. "Son, I walked away from God a long time ago, and a lot of it had to do with Carrie's death. I'm so sorry I never told you about her. I'm also sorry for asking Nana and Grandpa to never mention her to you. She was this beautiful and lively girl. I never thought I'd have to say goodbye to her so soon."

"Dad, we can talk about this a different time. I'm in no rush."

"Don't mind these tears. They've been bottled up for so long, it actually feels good to finally release them." He chuckled. Drew was happy at his response. He was anxious to hear more about his friend-turned-aunt Carrie.

"It was the summer of 1990. I was 17 and had just graduated high school... Carrie was 12. Mama and Daddy were gone for the afternoon, and it was always understood that I was in charge while they were away. She was bored inside and asked if I would take her horseback riding. So I did. Well, we didn't ride for long because it was so hot and humid. We put the horse away in the stable and started walking back toward the house. As we got closer to the big oak tree, a blue butterfly flew right past us. Carrie started jumping and pointing like she had just spotted a million dollars. She forgot how hot it was and started following the butterfly. She said, 'Oh Beanie, I've gotta get closer to her and just maybe she'll let me hold her.' The butterfly flew high into the tree, so she started climbing. I yelled at her to get down. Not only was it too hot, but the butterfly had landed too high in the tree for her to climb. She climbed higher, though, and said, 'I've gotta get up close to that butterfly Beanie! That species of butterfly shouldn't even be here. It's native to South America.' I'm going inside, I said to her. 'Oh just wait for me why don't you?' I told her she was being hard headed and that I wasn't going to bake in the sun and watch her fall from the tree. She said, 'Fine! Go in then.' I did, but I watched her from the kitchen window climb all the way up to that butterfly. She was so excited, because she'd gotten so close that the butterfly landed on her finger. But the branch that she crawled onto was weak and couldn't support her." He paused and wiped more tears. "I watched her as she fell to her death. I rushed outside screaming her name, but it was too late. She was gone. She died holding that Blue Morph butterfly in her hand."

"I have played it over and over in my mind how that day could've ended differently. I could've demanded we stay inside because it was too hot. I could've pulled her down from the tree before she got too high. She would've been angry with me, but she would still be here. I could've forced her to go with Mama and Daddy, but I let her hang with me instead. I was responsible for her Drew and I let her die. That has been a hard pill to swallow.

I thought I was over her death. I thought I'd let myself off the hook. In reality, though, I just brushed all of it under the rug. But when Sophia was born, it apparently exposed all my unresolved issues. The older she gets, the more she looks like Carrie. The more she looks like Carrie, the angrier I've gotten with you.

"Why? I don't understand."

"When I look at you, it's like I'm looking at myself when I was a boy. And I'm so angry with that boy because he didn't save his little sister."

"Wow! That's deep!"

I know it all sounds weird, but apparently that's why I've been so distant from you all these months. You've done nothing wrong. I'm what's wrong, and I'm sorry." He gave Drew a long embrace.

"It's okay Dad. But she doesn't blame you. I remember something she said to me while we were sitting in the big tree in Heaven. She said that our decisions have consequences and that sometimes the outcome is good, but sometimes it's not. I didn't know it then, but she was talking about her decision to climb the tree."

"She told you that?"

"Yep, she sure did. And she wasn't sad when she said it. She has no worries up there. She's just fine with God, all her butterflies, and her horses. She just wants her big brother to be okay down here."

He sat there with his head down. Then he turned to Drew and said, "So you really saw her, huh!"

Drew nodded, as if to say "for the millionth time, yes!"

"Unbelievable!" His dad shook his head in amazement. "What was she wearing?"

"A blue and white sundress; white at the top, light blue in the middle and then dark blue on bottom. She wore blue leggings. I think that's what they call them. She had brown combat-like boots on that laced up in the front." Drew smiled as he recalled her attire.

"Goodness! This is too much! Way too much! That's what she was wearing the day she died. You really did see her in your dream!"

Drew's smile faded, and he lowered his head. "You still don't believe I was actually there, huh?" Andrew Sr. wished he could take back the statement.

"Son, this has been hard for me to take in. This stuff doesn't happen normally. Maybe I'll get there one day. But my mind just won't let me accept it right now. Just bear with me, okay."

Drew nodded. His father was starting to make him doubt as well. But he quickly dismissed the thought from his mind. "So what's this?" Drew was looking at the box.

"Nana gave me this box. It has a few of Carrie's things inside. All these years, I've never had the strength to open it. I've tried, Lots of times." He paused, as if remembering something. "I used to have all these nightmares about her falling. They stopped for a while, but when Sophia was born they started up again. Every time I jumped up from the nightmare, I'd get up and pull this box from the attic. I thought if I opened the box, the nightmares would go away. But I just couldn't bring myself to opening this darn thing. So I'd just sit on the floor beside it and cry."

"Yeah, I heard you."

"You did? I'm sorry son."

"No, it's alright. I thought you were a ghost!"

"A ghost?" He offered a muffled chuckle.

"Yeah. Never mind where I got that from. But glad it was you though. I mean I'm sorry for why you were crying. I'm just glad the sounds were not a ghost."

"Alright. Well, there's no better time than now to open this thing. Don't you think?" His heart raced. *Don't open the box Andrew! Just forget about her!* Drew watched him shaking his head, as if he was having some private conversation with someone, and the answer was no.

"Yes Dad, let's do it together. God will be our strength!"

Immediately after Carrie's funeral, when all the guests had left their home, Andrew Sr. told his parents that if they wanted him to come home from college to visit, they would have to remove all memories of Carrie from plain site. Her memory would be too much to handle, he'd told them. His mother had begged him to seek grief counseling, but he refused. He said that therapy was for wimps; that talking about his dead sister wouldn't bring her back, nor would it ease the guilt of not being there when she fell from the tree.

His parents figured they'd just lost one child. They didn't want to lose another, so they complied with his demands. They removed all traces of her from open areas. That meant pictures had to be removed from the living room walls, off the mantle, and from hallways of their home. They reluctantly placed them in her bedroom and in the attic. But Nana packed one box especially for Andrew in hopes that, one day, he'd open it, reconcile his emotions, and honor her memory. She was grateful that he didn't refuse it.

So here he was again, attempting to open the box after many failed attempts. This time was different though. Carrie had spoken to him from beyond the grave. He could no longer ignore the box nor the emotions associated with her death. He took a deep breath, then proceeded to cut through the thick layers of tape that held the contents of Carrie Carmichael, the butterfly whisperer. He laid the scoring knife down almost in slow motion and parted the flaps of the box. The ritual was like exhuming her casket then opening it to reveal the painful contents.

The first thing that his shaking hand pulled out was a framed baby picture of Carrie. He and Drew both stared at it in silence. There was an uncanny resemblance to baby Sophia– the eyes, the lashes, the cheekbones. He placed the picture beside the box and pulled out a photo album of her. Andrew Sr. opened it then began explaining to his son the particulars of each picture on every page. They both looked, laughed, and wiped away tears–mostly Andrew Sr. The next thing that was pulled out was a large brown envelope. In it contained all of her school report cards and awards. She was an outstanding student who had never made anything less than a grade of "A" on her report cards. Andrew remembered how driven she was to do well, always reading or creating games to make studying fun at home. He knew that her future was promising but it came to an abrupt end that hot Saturday afternoon when he failed her. Andrew Sr. shook his head, and continued exploring the contents of the box. He pulled a VHS videotape out that was labeled Happy Birthday Beanie.

"You wanna see what's on it?"

Drew shook his head in affirmation. Andrew Sr. got up and went in search of the only VHS player that remained in the Carmichael home. He located it in their closet then eagerly connected it to the bedroom television. Drew sat on the floor near the player to push the buttons because there was no remote control. He pressed rewind and the tape spun loudly to the beginning. Just then, Karen knocked on the door and peeked her head inside.

"May I come in?"

"Sure love!" He motioned for her to join him on the sofa. "We found a video inside the box. We're about to take a look at it." She walked over, kissed his cheek, and set snugly next to him. The tape stopped. Drew looked back at his Dad.

"I'm gonna press the play button now, okay?"

"Alright son." Andrew took a deep breath, then exhaled. Every breath he'd taken after his collapse somehow felt different. Easier. Brand new.

A girl, appearing to be approximately 12 years old stood very close to the video camera. She giggled, and said "Big brothers are supposed to be a pain. Big brothers are supposed to get on your last nerve. Little sisters are supposed to wish they turn into lizards and just... slither away! But not my big brother! Oh no, he's not the slithering kind! He's awesome!!! He's beyond awesome! I mean, who takes their little sister with them to hang out with friends? BEANIE DOES! What 16 year old brother reads stories to his little sister right before bedtime? BEANIE DOES! What big brother makes sure his little sis brushes her teeth and says her prayers before bed? BEANIE DOES! Some call him Andrew Carmichael... He's Beanie to me... my incredible big brother who I'm proud to have ALL to myself! So Beanie, although I can't sing a lick, I love you enough to make a fool of myself, right here and right now. Because it's your 17th birthday and I love you immensely! So here goes!!!"

She backs away from the camera, and the camera operator zooms in as she walks to the piano. She sits on the piano stool and starts to play. "Happy birthday to you. Happy birthday to you. Happy birthday my Beanie. Happy birthday to you!" She continues playing the ending to the song, then she looks at the camera and winks! "Happy Birthday Beanie! I'm gonna miss you something terrible when you leave for college!"

She forces a pout, then blows a kiss to the camera. "I love you!" The television went to fuzz!

Drew pressed rewind. "I need to see it again!" He pushed play when it was time then moved closer to the TV knowing that this was as close he'd ever get to her now; at least until he saw her again in Heaven. After it played a second time, they all just sat there. Moments passed before Drew eventually turned from the TV and toward his parents. Andrew Sr. was visibly shaken, but felt relief in allowing his tears to visibly fall instead of those quick releases near the attic beside the box.

"Mom did you ever meet her?"

"No, I didn't. Only heard about her." She paused for a moment, then continued. "Drew, I'm thankful that you had this... uhmm... experience last night. It's been a really tough day, but I'm sure that our days moving forward will be brighter."

Wow, she's a non-believer too! Drew thought. She just dunked the word "experience" in a bucket full of doubt. Drew felt insulted, after all he'd shared with them today. He started to doubt himself again. Yesterday was probably the toughest day of his life and the kick from Luke did cause him to hit his head really hard on the ground. Perhaps the combination of the head trauma and the mental anguish caused his very delusional dream.

Then suddenly, his eyes widened. Without a word, he dashed out of their room and bolted upstairs. Karen shrugged her shoulders then leaned over to Andrew Sr. and gave him a hug. "Remind me to schedule a doctor's appointment for him on Monday."

"Why do you say that?"

"Because whatever happened to him at school yesterday has caused this boy's dreams to tap into some supernatural realm. I've never seen anything like this in all my days. Simply amazing! Or... do you think perhaps he's talked to your mother?"

"I've already called her. She swears that she's never uttered a word about Carrie to him."

"Hmmm! So again, I'll be calling Dr. Craven's office first thing Monday morning." She laughed trying to lighten the mood. Andrew Sr. didn't join in. A portion of him desperately wanted to believe.

"So Karen, how do we explain him raising that heavy window alone? I even checked the alarm system. It should've gone off when it was raised, but it didn't."

Drew returned, interrupting the conversation. He stood before them excitedly, holding the white shirt he'd worn the day before in his hand. The smile and tears streaming down his face had them worried. They feared their boat was about to tip over again.

"I know that I have warped your brains today, but just hear me out one more time. It really makes sense to me why you wanna believe that everything I told you was just a dream. Shucks, you almost had me convinced a few minutes ago! But I'm so glad I remembered something! Drew picked up the medicine bottle that sat beside the box and handed it to his dad. "You might wanna take some more of this so that you don't pass out again." Andrew accepted the bottle, but with hesitation.

"Something amazing happened to me last night and I refuse to let you all go to bed thinking that your son has lost his mind, because I haven't!" Karen grabbed her husband's hand, fearful of what was to come. "Dad, you and Carrie were very close, I imagine. Is that true?"

"Yeah, we were."

"Well, I know it's been a while, but do you remember what her favorite perfume was?" Andrew Sr.'s heart rhythm had increased in pace.

"Uhh... it was called... uhh... something Patches. She wore it all the time."

Drew helped him out. "It was called Sweet Patches!"

"Sweet Patches! That's right!"

"Well guess what! She's still wearing that same perfume in Heaven! When I hugged her last night, it got all over my shirt." Drew handed the shirt to his dad. His hands trembled as he slowly lifted it to his nose. He took in a deep whiff and immediately began sobbing.

Mom, here's a memento for you too." Drew dug into his pants pocket, then pulled out the moon rock God had thrown to him. He tossed it to her. When it touched her hands, she felt God's spirit. "Ball's in your court now!" He smiled. "That's what God said to me when He threw it to me!

"Last night was not a dream, Okay! I had a real meeting on the moon with God, our Creator. There was so much I didn't understand during that meeting, but most of it makes so much sense now." He paused before continuing. "God still loves you after all these years you've ignored Him and He's still waiting for the two of you to return to Him. I hope you do that soon, because I'd like for our entire family to praise Him together, starting in the morning at church. It's where I wanna be. I want my little sister to learn about God in church too, just like Carrie did. Will you take us?"

Both his parents nodded as if in a trance.

"Ok then, great!" He wiped his face with the back of his hand.

"Can I have my shirt back now?"

"Let me hold on to it just tonight... if you don't mind."

"That's fine Dad. Matter of fact, just keep it. I understand. I only spent a little while with Carrie, and I miss her. I can only imagine how you've felt all these years. It's been one long and emotional day. I'm going up to my room now. Good night guys." His parents nodded again, still speechless. Drew looked back and said, "A miracle happened to your boy last

night! I had a meeting on the moon with God! How
cool is that?" He winked at them, then exited.

Spring 2010

CHAPTER THIRTEEN

A ministry assistant at New Birth Christian Center escorted the morning speaker and his family to the guest chamber. The atmosphere in the room was very different from the cold and brightly lit hallway that led them there. There were plush leather sofas on either side of this dimly lit room. The electric fireplace on the back wall of the room welcomed its guests. A flat screen TV floated above it. On either side of the fireplace were bookshelves complete with bibles and other spiritual reads.

"Please make yourselves comfortable while you wait for service to start. Over here to the left is a table of refreshments complete with fruit, pastries, coffee, and juice. Help yourselves to whatever. Drew, over here to the right is a desk area, just in case you want to look over or make changes to your message. Family, when he is ready for some alone time, and that is highly encouraged, you all can retreat into this separate area this way. Follow me."

Beyond the refreshment table was a door that led into another room, outfitted like the first, except smaller.

"It is now 9:20; I'll be back at 10:00 to seat all of you. Then Andrew, I will return for you shortly thereafter. Will that work?" She smiled, not expecting anyone to object to the schedule.

"The restrooms are right across the hall, and my office is immediately beside it. If you need me for anything, just let me know." She exited.

Nana and Grandpa went immediately for the coffee. Karen poured hot water to steep tea. Andrew Sr. grabbed a bottle of water. Any other day, the pastries would have excited Drew, but not this day. He had a message to deliver to a large congregation of about 2,000. He decided on orange juice for the moment.

"So proud of you, grandson!" Nana said, as she landed a kiss on his forehead. "So proud!"

"Thanks Nana!"

"And you're looking quite handsome, too!" she doted.

Andrew Sr. had taken Drew shopping a few weeks before to buy a special suit. He selected a black suit, a white dress shirt, and a black tie.

After a few minutes of light chatter, the family retreated next door leaving Drew to collect his thoughts. He placed his bible and portfolio onto the desk, then he plopped down onto the closest sofa. He propped his feet up on the ottoman and smiled as he looked around. *I could get use to this,* he thought. As he admired the abstract painting on the opposing wall, his mind recalled the interesting turn of events that had landed him in that very spot. *And to think, it all started with one bully.* He shook his head.

Drew thought back to that Monday morning conference at Sterling Creek Elementary to discuss the bully situation. Mrs. Baxter had called Karen to inform her that it wasn't necessary to bring Drew to school on time. "Just bring him when you all arrive for the meeting at 10:30", she'd said. They wanted to make sure there would be no further interaction between Luke and Drew. It was all part of the school's action plan to address an outcry of bullying.

The meeting had included Mrs. Baxter, Ms. Crane, Andrew Sr., Karen, the school counselor, Mrs. Davenport, and Drew. He sat between his parents and Mrs. Baxter sat directly across from them. Mrs. Davenport and Ms. Crane sat on opposite sides of her. His composition book sat before Ms. Crane, open to the page of his fake article about his murder. "Is that it?" Karen asked Ms. Crane. She nodded and slid it across the table to her. Everyone was quiet while she read it silently to herself.

October 28, 2008

"11-Year-Old Bully Kills Boy At School"

TEXAS — An 11 year old boy has been charged with murder after the beating death of another student in the small town of Solome near Houston, authorities said.

The juvenile ~~murderer~~ suspect, Luke Hermann, is accused of beating to death fellow student Andrew

Carmichael Jr. at Sterling Creek Elementary. Carmichael suffered broken ribs and internal bleeding from the brutal bashing that lead led to his death. The ~~accident~~ incident occurred during recess. By the time teachers were alerted, it was too late.

Hermann, who reportedly confessed to the assault, was immediately detained by school officials, and was later charged with murder.

Friends of Andrew told reporters that Luke was an angry kid who frequently picked on Andrew, but they didn't know why. One friend described the victim as a Straight-A student, great athlete, an avid reader, and was well liked by many of his peers. This murder comes as a big shock to the small town of Solome, TX. Carmichael, who loved science, aspired to one day become ~~a scientist~~ an astronaut. He leaves to mourn his parents, Andrew Sr. and Karen Carmichael, and 15 month old sister, Sophia.

Karen slid it to Andrew Sr. as she wiped her falling tears. After he looked up, signaling that he was done reading it, Mrs. Baxter started the meeting. "Good morning Andrew."

"Good morning."

"I want you to know that you are not in any trouble, okay."

"Yes ma'am."

"And we won't be frightened by anything that you have to share with us regarding the matter we're here. We only want to know what happened to you and for how long. It'll help us adults decide what we need to do from this point forward to help you and other students. Is that fair?

"Yes ma'am."

Mrs. Baxter looked at Ms. Crane, giving her the signal to speak.

"Andrew, I read your journal entry about... about your murder. I read it over the weekend and that is why we're here. Can you tell us why you wrote it?"

Here we go again, Drew thought. "I wrote it because that's how I felt my life was going to end."

The adults looked at each other, wondering what the next question should be.

"Did you write it because Luke Hermann had in fact been bullying you?" Mrs. Baxter asked.

"Yes, ma'am."

"Can you tell us when it started?"

"It started the second week of school." Drew noticed that Mrs. Davenport was writing everything that he said.

"How often were you bullied by him?"

"Uhmmm... maybe 1-3 times a week."

"Can you give us specifics? Like, what did he do to you?"

Drew looked up at Mrs. Baxter, his interviewer, then scanned the table to meet the eyes of the others. They were all thirsty for details. Then Drew looked back at his hands that were intertwined atop the table. "Luke hurt me. He hurt me with his words and with his hands. Sometimes with his feet even."

"Andrew, can you think of a particular time that he hurt you?"

"Yes. I remember all the times that Luke hurt me."

"Well, let's start with just one. What did he do?"

Silence.

"Andrew, are you nervous?" Ms. Crane asked.

"No ma'am. Not nervous."

"Well, dear heart we need to know what Luke did to you." Ms. Crane pleaded.

He paused for a moment, then he started to speak.

"A couple days ago, a very important person helped me understand that hurting people hurt people. So if that's true, then it would be a good idea to see what's hurting Luke. Maybe he won't hurt people anymore. I'm sorry, but I don't want to tell you all the things he did to me. But it is true; he hurt me. He hurt me a lot... and I thought I was going to die."

"You sound as if you don't feel that way anymore," said Mrs. Davenport.

"I don't." He answered confidently.

"What has changed since you wrote this?"

How to answer them... how to answer them? Drew looked up at his parents who offered encouraging smiles.

"I had an encounter with God, and He assured me that Luke would not harm me anymore."

Mrs. Baxter met the eyes of his parents, not sure what to say. She wasn't expecting that response from Drew. She cleared her throat.

"Well Drew, when I met with your parents earlier before we brought you in, I shared with them some information I think you'll be glad to hear. Luke Hermann will not be attending Sterling Creek any longer. Just this morning, an official from social services withdrew him from this school. He'll be attending whatever school is closest to the new home that they find for him."

Drew smiled. *He told the truth!*

"You don't have to worry about him anymore; He's gone! However, the details of what he did to you can be sent to social services so that they can better handle him. And just maybe if your parents want to seek justice for you by telling the police what he did, then they can."

Silence.

"Drew?"

"Yes ma'am, I hear you." He paused momentarily, then continued. "Please tell the new people that the kid that Luke hurt forgives him. Ask them to give him a chance and to help him with his problems so that he can be a happy kid again. I know what he did was wrong, but he needs help. That's all I really want for him."

Mrs. Baxter was stunned. Where does this kid get such compassion? She wondered. Ms. Crane had lowered her head in a poor attempt to coax the lump in her throat and reverse the tears that clouded her vision. She felt guilty for missing the signs that were so obvious to her now. Mrs. Davenport dropped her pen and just looked at Drew in wonderment. How much counseling could she offer to a kid who sounded like he was alright? Karen glanced over at Andrew Sr. as they listened to their son, who did not sound like his normal self. This was some new and improved kid.

The meeting went on for a while longer, and came to an end shortly after 11:30. Drew gave his parents a hug, then walked to class 503 alongside Ms. Crane. There was something special about this kid that made her feel proud to have him in her class. She secretly hoped, in the days to come, that he'd share more about his God encounter.

Luke Hermann remained the hot topic at the school for weeks. No one knew what really became of him, but several theories circulated during lunch and at recess.

"My brother told me that his friend told him that Luke went to prison."

"It's probably because of the gang I heard he joined."

"I heard that Luke's white stepdad hated him because he was half white, half black. So he beat him up and put him in the hospital."

"Well, I heard he died."

The rumors went on for weeks and months. Eventually, the students of Sterling Creek Elementary spoke less of him. He became a thing of the past. History.

Then, Drew remembered how his father had courageously started therapy to deal with his past and to help heal his bruised relationship with his son. Things between them were back to normal. Drew was pleased, especially with the new father-son outings that included trips to the science museum and local arcade. The atmosphere at home was even different. It was like a heavy spirit had been lifted. But what Drew loved the most was his parent's commitment to taking them to church that Sunday after the meeting on the moon. He was especially proud of his dad who led the family to the front of the church to join New Birth Christian Center that same day. They'd been regulars ever since.

Drew walked over to the desk in the guest chamber, and flipped through his prepared message. He'd studied it so many times over the last six weeks, he could recite it without looking. He closed it, running his hand along the front of the faux leather portfolio.

He thought about that particular bible study where he couldn't help but share a small portion of his conversation he'd had with God. The bible study leader was so moved, that he took Drew to Pastor Green's office, so that he could tell him as well. When Drew was done, the pastor set back in his over-sized leather chair, to ponder what he'd just heard. "Son, it's apparent to me that you have a special anointing on your life.

"Sir, I'm not really sure what you mean."

"What I mean is that you have been called to be a special ambassador for God. He has shared some things with you that apparently He wants you to share with His people."

"Yes sir, he told me that."

"Did He now?"

"Yes, sir."

"Well, we'll have to see about making that happen. Let your parents know that I'll be contacting them soon. God bless you young man."

Drew was eventually given the invitation to speak at a Sunday morning service at New Birth. Not just any service either. Pastor Green had invited him to be the special guest speaker on Easter Sunday when the church would be busting at the seam with the regular attendees and the flock of special occasion worshippers. "The people need a fresh word from God. Andrew will be the perfect person to deliver that word." Pastor Green had told Andrew Sr.

"Doesn't he need special training or a special license to deliver a sermon?"

"Brother Carmichael, if God gave Drew a message to deliver, then that is his license. It's better than any license that man could ever offer."

A knock at the guest chamber door interrupted Drew's thoughts. The ministry assistant poked her head inside. "Hi there. May I come in?"

"Of course."

"It's time for me to take your family to their seats now."

"Okay."

Drew alerted them, and they each filed into the main chamber where he was.

"I'm proud of you, son" Andrew Sr. said as he hugged Drew. "I'll be praying for you while you speak, okay. You're gonna do well."

"Thanks Dad."

Karen put Sophia down, then she gave her boy a long embrace. She straightened his tie. "Your Mama's proud of you too. You know that, right?"

"I know."

"We're leaving, but I want you to have this, just in case you get nervous out there." It was the rock from the moon.

"Thanks Mom!" He slid it into his pocket.

Nana and Grandpa stole quick hugs as they all exited into the brightly lit hallway. The door closed behind them and Drew breathed a sigh of relief. He went over to the refreshment table and ate a few of the purple grapes. He walked back over to the desk, figuring by the time he read his message one last time, it would be time to be escorted into the sanctuary. He was ready.

CHAPTER FOURTEEN

D rew approached the podium and glanced out into the large crowd staring back at him. *God's people*, he thought. He smiled when he saw his family seated on the front row of the far right aisle. Just as he looked away, he did a double take, believing he saw Carrie sitting on his father's lap. But smiling and waving at him was Carrie's twin, little Sophia. *Is she playing tricks on me all the way from Heaven?* He laughed, in spite of himself. Then he saw Matthew and his family. They were seated on the third row of the center aisle. He wanted to wave, but figured he better not. He looked passed them and saw a sea of hats worn by some of the ladies of the church. The children were adorned in frilly pinks and polyester blue outfits purchased the day before. The younger ones held their Easter baskets in their laps, admiring all the sugary contents. The men wore their fine suits with pastel ties and neatly folded handkerchiefs. It was a Sunday morning fashion show minus the runway.

"Good morning New Birth Christian family, and good morning visitors. You guys look nice out there... and you smell good too!" The crowd chuckled.

"Happy Resurrection Sunday! You know, the last time I gave a speech, it was in front of 27 students at my school. Today, it looks like I'm speaking to 10,000 people! What a big difference. But I'm okay with that, because I have a story to share this morning, and it excites me more than anything!

"My name is Andrew James Carmichael, Jr. and I'm 13 years old. I'd like to think of myself as an average kid, but 2 years ago, when I was 11, my life didn't seem so normal. I thought I was going to die. For weeks, I had been tormented by a bully at my school. And although that was the scariest time of my life, I don't think I'd be standing before you today if I didn't go through that experience. You see, I didn't know God well, but I had been taught to pray to Him. When the torture got really bad, I poured my heart out to Him in prayer. Then God met me in a miraculous way and helped me with my problems. During my meeting with Him, He told me to deliver a message to you, His people, whom He loves. I won't be able to share it all today, but I will focus on one subject that God talked to me about—forgiveness."

Luke Hermann was long gone from Solome, but Drew shared only bits and pieces of his painful experience with the congregation. It wouldn't be right, he thought, for people to harshly judge Luke when they didn't know his full story. All they needed to know was that he hurt him often, and that he thought he was going to die by Luke's hands.

"On the night that I met God, He said to tell you that bullies come in all forms, and that you will certainly encounter them at some point in your life. They're not just in schools like mine was. A bully can be a family member in your home, a co-worker at your job, a neighbor, or even a church member. But no matter who they are, they are still people who have a story to tell. If you're lucky, you may learn of their story, but most times you won't. No matter how the problem is addressed or resolved, God said to forgive them. That also means we must forgive ourselves for things we've done wrong or for things we believe we've done wrong." He glanced at his father. "Let yourself off the hook and move on," he continued.

"God said to tell you to become more magnanimous. Say it after me. "Mag-nan-i-mus." The congregation obeyed.

"Magnanimous! It means to generously forgive people and to not seek revenge or be resentful to those who've done you wrong.

"Magnanimous! It means having the courage to take the high road when faced with difficult people or situations.

"When we are magnanimous, we interrupt the toxic energy that's in the atmosphere, keeping it from connecting with our spirit making us toxic and cantankerous.

"When we are magnanimous, we help people. We impact their story and even our own. We may not ever see when the other person's story changes, but it does. God said so. I often wonder what happened to the boy who bullied me, but no matter what, I'm so glad that I forgave him for what he did to me, and I pray that he's doing okay.

"When we are magnanimous, we represent God well. He said people who have a problem forgiving should examine their relationship with Him. The closer that we are to Him, the easier it is to forgive.

"For you nicely dressed, good smelling people out there who are wondering why this kid is speaking about forgiveness on Resurrection Sunday," Drew paused. "Well, there is a very good reason."

"On the night that I met God, He said to remind His people that we are all sinners. That's why He allowed His Son, Jesus Christ, to be crucified on the cross so that our sins would be forgiven when we asked. That very same sacrifice was not just for me or for you, but also for those who hurt us as well. So if God forgives the person who has caused harm, He expects us to do the very same thing.

"Parents, it might be somewhat difficult for you to hear advice coming from a 13 year old kid, so ignore me—the messenger, but please listen to the message. You *must* take excellent care of yourselves both physically and emotionally. Exercise and deal with your problems, because when you do, your children will feel peace and love inside their home. When children feel peace and love inside their home, they naturally become more self-confident. Then, when you bring them to church on Sundays to learn about God, they will grow up nurturing a true relationship with Him. Children who receive the gift of self-confidence from home and who have a true relationship with God usually don't grow up to become bullies. The God-confidence within them won't allow bullies to trample all over them. They will walk tall and boldly, knowing that Abba, our Father, our Daddy, will guide and protect them all the days of their lives. The atmosphere will change when they walk into a room, and they will be quick to forgive. So parents, take good care of yourselves for your children's sake... and bring them here often. They deserve it. God requires it.

"To all you kids out there, thank your parents for bringing you here today. You all could've been at home, but you're here to celebrate the death and resurrection of our Savior, Jesus Christ! So thank them now." The young congregants clapped their hands.

"Finally young people, please hear me. Hear me loud and clear! Being bullied is NOT okay! If someone is hurting you by saying mean things to you, or if they are somehow causing pain to your body, you do NOT have to keep it a secret. Even if that person tells you that you better keep quiet or something bad will happen to you, I urge you to take the T3 oath: *Tell The Truth* anyways! Tell an adult that you trust, like your parents or a teacher, so that you can get the help you deserve. The other person might get in trouble, but they can also get help too, so they won't hurt anyone else. You don't have to suffer pain from a bully. End it before it gets worse. I'm almost done this morning, but I'd like all school-aged children to please stand and repeat these vows after me.

"I won't bully!"

"I won't bully!" The crowd echoed.

"I won't be bullied!"

"I won't be bullied!"

"I will T3—tell the truth!"

"I will T3—tell the truth!"

"Thank you! You may be seated.

"I've shared my story. I've shared a bit of His story. What's your story? Does it look like mine before I met God? Lost, scared, confused, no peace? If you haven't met Him, it's not too late. Today is a great day to learn more about Him. He's waiting for you. For those that have met Him, but walked away for some reason, He told me to tell you that He still loves you, and He's waiting for your return. It doesn't matter what you've said or done. He said your peace offering, Jesus Christ, died on the cross and rose again for all our sins to be forgiven. He wants all who are not in relationship with Him to just come. He already knows your story, but He wants you to tell it to Him. So come! Pastor Green is here to extend the invitation."

Drew took a seat, and wiped his face with the handkerchief that he pulled from his pocket. The congregation stood to their feet and clapped loud and long. Some cried, as they lifted their hands in the air praising God for speaking to their hearts. Drew's family stood as well, except for Andrew Sr., who was too overcome by emotion. He covered his face, but his tears found escape routes to run free.

Just as Pastor Green was about to extend the invitation to salvation, he was startled by someone in the audience who appeared in a hurry to exit his pew. Instead of heading toward the exit doors, this person walked eagerly down the left aisle toward the pulpit. The thunderous applause continued, believing the young visitor had come to accept God as his Lord and Savior. He stood before the pulpit, and locked eyes with Pastor Green. Curious, Pastor Green walked down to shake the fella's hand. He wore dark grey dress pants, and a white starched dress shirt. His hair appeared freshly cut, faded on the sides while the thick natural curls lay free atop his head. He wore black rimmed glasses, providing a nice contrast to his hazel eyes. He had something to say, but he whispered into Pastor Green's ear first. The loud praise mellowed, and the congregation anxiously waited to hear what need this person might have. Surely Pastor Green would share what the issue was.

Drew slowly snapped out of his after-speech stupor, and turned his attention toward the main attraction, Pastor Green and the well-dressed young man talking to him. Pastor Green turned to glance at Drew for a moment, as he contemplated his next action. Then finally, after what felt like forever to the congregation and now Drew, Pastor Green lifted his head to engage the congregation.

"Let the church say Amen."

"Amen." They all replied in unison.

"If you can, please, please, take your seats. Thank you so kindly. In all my years of pastoring, I can honestly say that I have never witnessed a service quite like this. Our God is so amazing, and He deserves our highest praise!" The congregation collectively said Amen again.

"We have just heard our own, Brother Andrew give a heartfelt testimony about being bullied at school, and how that experience led him to experience God in such a miraculous way. Some of you might be doubtful of his experience, but if you believe that there is a God, you must also believe that He can do whatever He desires, whenever He chooses. Amen."

"We have a visitor today who has something special to share and I find it quite befitting that he shares it before all of you."

Drew sat up more in his chair so that he could hear what this visitor had to say.

"Uh… hello everyone. I used to live here in Solome, but now I live in Georgia with my dad. We came to town to take care of some business, but, uh, I told my dad that I needed to see someone before we left. I needed to tell him something. Then yesterday, we found out that the person I needed to talk to would be speaking here today. My name is Luke Hermann, and I was the bully that Drew was talking about in his speech."

There was a loud collective gasp by the congregation. Drew instinctively jumped to his feet, and so did his best friend and bodyguard Matthew. Momentarily, Drew's brain rewound back to that time when he was a frightened 11 year old. It was the first time he grabbed for the moon rock that was in his right pocket. Then he heard a soft whisper in his ear. "He won't hurt you again, remember?" Drew calmed his breathing, and stared at this kid who did not look anything like his former perpetrator. He looked clean and was a little taller. He certainly didn't appear as if he'd returned to carry out a death sentence.

"When I lived here, I was a troubled kid. No, I was actually a monster! My mom married a drunk who hated me and he hurt me every chance he got. He convinced my mom to cut ties with everyone who loved us so we left Georgia and went into hiding for over four years. When my mom got sick, my stepdad started drinking more. When he drank more, he beat me more. Then when I went to school, I took my frustrations out on Drew. He had everything I didn't so I made him suffer. When I think about what I did to him, it makes me sad and ashamed." Luke shook his head.

"One day, we saw each other in the emergency room. I was there because my stepdad had broken my arm." The crowd groaned. "Instead of Drew ignoring me or walking away, he came over to me and forgave me for every mean thing that I had done to him. He even told me that God loved me, and that I was going to be okay. He encouraged me to tell the truth to the emergency room people. I didn't deserve all that, yet he showed me the love and forgiveness that he preached about today. That was the last time I saw Drew. That same day, my stepdad was arrested, and I was taken to a safe home until social services could find my dad."

Luke turned his back to the congregation, and looked directly at the guest speaker. "Drew, man, I've been waiting to tell you this for a very long time. I am so, so sorry!

Drew walked up to the podium and grabbed the extra microphone. "It's okay. I forgave you, remember?"

"Yeah, I know. But if I could take it all back, I would in a heartbeat. You didn't deserve any of it."

"Neither did you."

"Thank you for sharing God with me. Because you were being man... man... nan... what's that word you said?

"Magnanimous."

"Yes. Because you were being *that* word, you helped change my story for the better. My mom went on to Heaven, but I now live with my real dad, step mom, and 2 year old brother. My therapist says that I'm progressing well, that I can probably finish my sessions with her real soon. I'm still working on a lot of things, but I am proud to say that I'm no longer that bully. Thanks for showing me love in the emergency room that day." He placed his right fist over his heart. "You will always have a special place right here!"

The church musicians had begun playing the melody to one of Drew's favorite songs, "More than Anything" by Lamar Campbell. The choir softly harmonized the lyrics. Luke had never heard it before, but the music touched him at his core, encouraging him to complete what was on his heart to say. He turned back to the congregation.

"Because of him," pointing back at Drew, "I'm a believer!" He then pointed at the wooden cross that was suspended from the ceiling above his head. Overwhelmed with emotion, Drew lifted both his hands in praise to God. Tears ran down his face. Many congregants stood to their feet shedding tears of joy because they too had survived their bully. Others released tears of sorrow, thinking of loved ones who weren't so lucky. Andrew Sr. had his eyes closed, grateful that God had not given up on him; thankful to God for helping him to forgive his younger self for not being there when Carrie fell; and joyful for a son who decided to pray, causing the script to change.

Luke continued. "Jesus hung and died for my sins and I'll be forever grateful. Thank you Reverend for letting me say something. Thank you Mr. and Mrs. Carmichael for inviting me here today. And God bless all of you."

Drew walked slowly from the pulpit, towards the one who'd made the start of his fifth grade year a living nightmare. By the time Luke had returned the microphone to Pastor Green, Drew was standing behind him, his heart beating at a normal pace. Luke turned to face him, and for the first time they shared the same space without the presence of anger or crippling fear. Their mouths were closed shut, but their eyes spoke what had already been communicated moments before. Drew's eyes told Luke how proud he was of him for telling the truth in the emergency room, and for boldly sharing his story that day. Luke's eyes told Drew how remorseful he was for the cruel things that he'd done and for the things he had planned to do. What Luke remembered but dared not utter to God's people was that two years back when he was eleven, he had a step-by-step plan to kill the morning's speaker at Sterling Creek Elementary. Drew's seemingly perfect life had mocked his own; therefore, Luke had devised a plan to put an end to it. However, his murderous plot had been interrupted that fateful Saturday morning. Interrupted by love. Interrupted by forgiveness. Drew extended his right hand towards Luke, but Luke countered the greeting by extending his arms. Still standing under the cross, they embraced each other like old childhood buddies would do at a class reunion.

God was there, and He was pleased.

Let all bitterness and wrath and anger and clamor and slander be put away from you, along with all malice. Be kind to one another, tenderhearted, forgiving one another, as God in Christ forgave you.

~(Ephesians 4:31–32)

CPSIA information can be obtained
at www.ICGtesting.com
Printed in the USA
LVHW08s0032310718
585378LV00001B/65/P